MINE!

Natalie Hyde

Scholastic Canada Ltd.
Toronto New York London Auckland Sydney
Mexico City New Delhi Hong Kong Buenos Aires

Scholastic Canada Ltd.
604 King Street West, Toronto, Ontario M5V 1E1, Canada

Scholastic Inc.
557 Broadway, New York, NY 10012, USA

Scholastic Australia Pty Limited
PO Box 579, Gosford, NSW 2250, Australia

Scholastic New Zealand Limited
Private Bag 94407, Botany, Manukau 2163, New Zealand

Scholastic Children's Books
Euston House, 24 Eversholt Street, London NW1 1DB, UK

www.scholastic.ca

Library and Archives Canada Cataloguing in Publication
Hyde, Natalie, 1963-, author
Mine! / Natalie Hyde.
Issued in print and electronic formats.
ISBN 978-1-4431-4660-9 (softcover).--ISBN 978-1-4431-4661-6 (HTML)
I. Title.
PS8615.Y44M56 2017   jC813'.6   C2017-901506-0
C2017-901507-9

6 5 4 3 2 1   Printed in Canada 139   17 18 19 20 21

MIX
Paper from
responsible sources
FSC
www.fsc.org   FSC® C103567

For Sheldon, who appreciates a sweet ride.

CHAPTER 1

THE NAME'S DIRK STARK

Moose snot is a real thing, you know. So are bogs deep enough to swallow a man whole, and mosquitoes the size of bats. Okay, maybe not as big as bats, but bigger than any mosquito I've ever seen. And I'm not kidding about the moose snot. I should know, seeing as it was running down my arm.

If you had told me one week ago that I'd be stranded up a tree, covered in moose snot with onions stinking up my pockets, I'd have thought you were nuts. One week ago I was sitting in our living room trying to concentrate on my favourite TV show, where contestants get knocked into water by padded bars and oversized boxing gloves as they try to get through an obstacle course. But I could barely hear their *umpfs* and *ows* as they went flying, because someone was pounding on our apartment door.

Now, I had lived here long enough to know that nobody good ever pounded on the door. Friends who wanted to hang with you and church ladies bringing around Christmas food hampers always knocked. Cops coming to take your dad away for the latest "Failure to Appear" and landlords looking for the rent always pounded with their fists. So I did my best to ignore it, but the incessant pounding was now accompanied by a lady's voice calling, "Mr. Dearing. Mr. Dearing! I need you to open the door right now."

I winced at the name. You know, sometimes I really hated being a Dearing. As far as I could tell, no one named Dearing ever amounted to anything. They were all losers. And I didn't want to be one of them. So I'd made a plan. When I turned eighteen, I was going to change my name. Did you know you could do that? Just pay some money and presto! chango! you had a new name. One that you *picked* — not one that your parents thought was cute or funny or unique.

I've decided on the name "Dirk Stark." I like how tough the name Dirk sounds. Not like Chris. Chris sounds all soft and mushy with that "s" on the end. A "Chris" sounded like someone weak, who was deathly afraid of small spaces and cried in secret. Someone named "Dirk" could crush pop cans with one hand and would stand up to bullies. No one would pick on someone named Dirk. And Stark, because, well, my favourite superhero is Iron Man, a.k.a. Tony Stark. I had to wait another five years until I was old enough, but then I would be Dirk Stark and say goodbye to Chris Dearing forever.

"Mr. Dearing. MR. DEARING! You need to answer this door!" The voice was getting pretty loud now. I knew who it was anyway. It had to be Mrs. Critch, the wife of the landlord. He always sent her to do the dirty work of collecting rent payments that were late. And ours usually was. I couldn't stand her. She was as thin as a stick and wore gobs of mascara, which made her look like an underfed zombie.

Best to get it over with because there is one truth about landlords — they never go away. Even if you stay really quiet and don't watch TV or squeak the floorboards, they know you're there and they'll keep hounding you until you talk to them.

I hurried to the kitchen. I had a secret hiding spot where I kept any money I found in my dad's wallet for rent. He needed help like that, otherwise there wouldn't be any money left. The one hundred dollars in there so far was a start and would get Mrs. Critch to leave, at least for a while. But when I looked in the English Break-fast Tea tin, it was empty.

Not good. It meant Dad had found my latest spot and I'd have to find another. That also meant he hadn't gone to work today like I'd hoped when I came home after school and he wasn't there. Down on Ainslie Street, near the warehouses, there is a place where men can go and look for work. Dock managers and construction foremen come around in vans looking for day labourers. It doesn't pay much but you can squeeze out enough for the rent if you work every day. Which he usually doesn't.

I went to the door and unlocked it. I kept the chain on, though. That was something Shard taught me when we moved here. Always keep the chain on when you are talking to someone at the door.

I opened it as far as the chain would allow and looked through the crack. It wasn't Mrs. Critch after all. It was someone I had never seen before. She was stuffed into a tan-coloured suit so tight it looked like it would burst at the seams the minute she moved. Her little piggy eyes were almost hidden by her puffy cheeks, and she was breathing hard.

"Are you Christopher Dearing?"

Five years from now I could say, "No, I'm not,"

but for today, I still was. Then it hit me: How did she know my name? She wasn't a tenant — I knew everyone who lived here. Other than Shard's family, they were pretty much all old people. This wasn't the best neighbourhood for raising a family. Maybe she was a distant relative of mine? I knew my dad's family pretty well, but not my mom's. They lived out west somewhere. My heart skipped a beat. Maybe this lady had a message from my mom.

I nodded, a lump in my throat.

"I'm from Family Services. The school board called me."

Uh oh. That couldn't be good. I shouldn't have admitted who I was. Shard would lecture me about that later, for sure.

"Why did they call you?" I asked.

"You've missed sixteen days in the last six months."

"Oh, my dad's been sick. I've been taking care of him." It was my usual answer when anyone asked me about missing school. And it wasn't even really a lie. Truth was I did have to look after my dad a lot these days.

"Can I speak to him?"

I looked over my shoulder at my father's empty bedroom.

"He's not well enough for visitors."

"It will only take a moment." The woman moved her pointy shoe forward like she was going to jam it between the door and the frame and stop me from closing it. A wave of panic washed over me, so I slammed the door shut and clicked the lock.

The banging started again.

"Christopher? Christopher, open the door. I need to speak to your father."

I just stood there, staring at the closed door and willing her to leave.

"Have it your way, Christopher. I'm coming back with the police."

CHAPTER 2

A JAGGED PIECE OF GLASS

Could she do that, I wondered? Could the police come and arrest me? Or my dad? I knew who would know the answer to that — Shard.

I listened to Mrs. Family Service's pointy shoes click down the hallway. I carefully cracked the door open again, terrified that she had tricked me and was still standing there. The hallway was empty. I ran down to Shard's apartment.

Now *there* was someone who got a cool name. I mean, really, Shard? Like a jagged piece of glass? No one is going to think you're a push-over with a name that means jagged piece of glass. No one. And her last name, Kent? Come on! Superman's name? You are invincible with the name Shard Kent, and this Shard is. Life just isn't fair.

Shard's younger sisters didn't luck out as much. Merle sounded like an old horse's name and Reese was almost as bad as Chris. They came to the door to gawk while I waited.

"Are you going to jail?" Merle asked.

"What are you talking about?"

"I heard that lady shouting that she was coming back with the police. Are they going to arrest you?" She had a look of excitement all over her face.

"No."

"Oh." The edges of her mouth drooped.

"They gonna toss the place?" Reese joined in, obviously wanting to cheer her sister up.

"You two watch too much TV. No one's getting arrested and no one's tossing anybody's place."

The two girls left me standing there, shooting me dirty looks as they walked away, for spoiling what would have been an exciting afternoon for them.

"Sorry," Shard said, coming to the door finally. "Cork needed changing."

There were times when I was glad to be an only child, and the thought of changing dirty diapers on a two-year-old brother made this one of those times.

"I need to talk to you," I told her.

"Come on, let's go to your place. Too crowded here."

When we were back in my apartment, I told her what happened.

"Can she really do that? Come back with the police, I mean. Am I really in trouble for skipping a few classes?"

"You don't want to mess with Family Services," Shard said. "They can stick you in foster care faster than you can blink."

"Foster care?" I couldn't believe they could do that because of a few missed days at school. "You're lying," I said.

That was the wrong thing to say. Shard's eyes narrowed and her hands balled into fists. She stomped over to me and only stopped when we were almost nose to nose.

"I. Don't. Lie."

I couldn't help it; I took a step back. Shard has a reputation, and it's not for being honest. It's for having a lightning-quick right hook. Rob Deegan knows exactly how quick it is — she broke his nose in grade five. If I remember correctly, it was for calling her a liar.

I took another step back.

"Sorry. Didn't mean it like that," I said, forcing myself not to protect my nose with my hands. "I just meant it seems like an overreaction for skipping school."

Shard relaxed her face and hands. "There's

probably more to it than just skipping school," she said. "Did your dad ever hit you?"

"No."

"He ever hit your mom?"

"No!"

Shard paused. "Has anyone at school been asking you questions?"

"Like what?"

"'Bout your mom?"

The French teacher at school asked a lot of questions when my mom disappeared. Questions I couldn't answer. "Yeah. Madame LaFarge."

"Did she ever comment on your clothes? Or your lunch? Or how tired or sick you looked?"

My heart started to speed up. She asked things like that all the time — about why I had a hole in my shirt, or where my lunch was, or why I had black circles under my eyes.

I nodded.

"That's it then. She's one of those do-gooders who thinks they're saving the world."

"Madame LaFarge called Family Services on us?"

Shard nodded. "Guaranteed. And now you've got trouble, 'cause once they start sniffing around, you're never safe."

Shard sounded like she knew what she was talking about. I remember a couple of years ago, her family had people in suits always coming and going from their place and Shard had been really stressed out. More than usual. Maybe someone had phoned Family Services on them too.

"So what do I do?"

"Well, for one, don't open the door to them. And how could you be so stupid as to admit who you are? Haven't I taught you anything?"

"I thought she had news from my mom," I mumbled.

"She still in the loony bin?"

"She's not in a loony bin!"

"Whatever. All you can do now is keep a low profile. Watch what you wear these last couple of days of the school year. Bring something to eat for lunch. And for Pete's sake, look healthy."

"Do you think she's coming back like she said? With the police?"

Shard nodded. "You'd better find your dad. And fast."

Great. Now I had to track down my dad and drag him out of some bar and get him back here before Mrs. Family Services returned with the cops. And then hope he was sober enough to convince them not to take me to a foster home. If the Dearings didn't have bad luck, they'd have no luck at all.

CHAPTER 3

THE TALE IS TOLD

Shard said she'd help me get my dad. I was glad. Sometimes I had trouble convincing him to leave a bar.

He hadn't always been like this. He used to be a master marine mechanic working on the ships down at the docks. He was the one they called when the tugboats blew an engine or even when the freighters had problems their own mechanics couldn't diagnose. He was that good.

Until he got fired.

"The fix is in" was what my mom said when I asked her why he lost his job. I didn't know what that meant. She said that it meant things were rigged behind the scenes.

I asked why they would do that to my dad. She said it was "because there is no room for an honest man down at the docks." She didn't think I saw, because she turned her head, but she was crying.

When I told her I was sure he'd get another job, she said, "Not if those thugs have anything to do with it."

That's all she would tell me. But she was right. After that, my dad couldn't find a job anywhere. He even applied to jobs in other cities all up and down both coasts. Shard filled me in on the rest. Her dad worked the cranes that unloaded the shipping containers. He said my dad reported that he saw some of the dockworkers unloading containers directly to trucks without them going through customs first. Her dad said that meant smuggling: drugs or even people. Something illegal. He also said that even the police must have been in on it, because not only was no one charged, there wasn't even an investigation. The only one who was punished was my dad, for squealing.

That's when the drinking started.

"Where do you think he is?" Shard asked, snapping me back to the present.

I thought for a moment. "With a hundred dollars in his pocket, he'll head to his favourite."

"The Bull?"

"Yup."

The Bull and Brambles liked to pretend it was an English pub. The trim outside was black and the frosted window on the door had gold-coloured curlicues all over it. Inside it was decorated with old horseshoes and British flags. My dad didn't go there because of the decorations, though. He went there because it was the only place that served his favourite beer, called Deadman's Creek. It was brewed in the Yukon, where my dad grew up, so I guess it reminded him of home.

Shard and I stopped inside the door of the Bull. It took a second or two for our eyes to adjust to the darkness. I don't know why bars are so dark even when the sun is shining. Maybe because the people inside like to feel like they're hidden away.

"What do you want?" a voice asked.

Fiona was standing behind the bar, scowling. As usual. She wasn't exactly the warm-and-fuzzy motherly type. Maybe you have to be tougher than most people when you are a bar owner. Or at least look tough. Fiona had *that* covered with her muscular frame and tattoos on both arms. Sure they were butterflies — but one had razor-sharp wings and the other had fangs. I shivered even though the air was warm and heavy inside.

"I'm looking for my dad," I said.

"You know you're not allowed to be in here, right?" Fiona said, then sighed. "He's holding court in the back." She tipped her head in the direction of a few tables that were in an area behind the bar. "Sounds like your dad's had quite the life — a stint in the French Foreign Legion, finding gold in the Yukon, his family's escape from Communist Europe . . ."

"He gets a little carried away when he's been drinking."

Fiona gave a little snort and kept wiping glasses with a ratty dishtowel.

Shard and I walked to the back.

"French Foreign Legion? What's that?" Shard asked.

"Soldiers who were paid to fight with the French army."

"Cool!" she said.

"Would be, if he had really joined."

"Oh."

"And for the record, my grandfather didn't strike it rich with a gold mine; he died penniless. And my ancestors aren't even *from* Europe. They came from Winnipeg."

Shard thought this was hilarious. I thought it was embarrassing. The Dearings led such lame lives that they had to make up histories to sound exciting and adventurous.

As we got closer, I heard my dad's unmistakably deep voice.

"Fifty . . . no a hunnert tousand dollars wort of gold, easy," he slurred.

We rounded the corner. My dad was sitting with two other guys at a table littered with dirty glasses.

"Man, you . . . you gotta go up der," one of the men said, pointing a finger at my dad. The other guy was trying to grab it and kept missing.

"I know, right?" my dad said. "Soon as I get my pension from the Legion, I'm outta here." My dad added a wave of his arm to show them how fast he would take off once that money arrived. What a joke. We were Dearings. We weren't going anywhere.

"Uh, Dad?" I plucked at his sleeve. My dad turned to me and made a face while he tried to focus his eyes.

"Dad, it's Chris. We've got to go home now."

Dad pulled his arm away. "I'm not finish here."

Fiona came over and stood behind me. "Yeah, prospector, you are. You've had enough for today."

She yanked my dad to his feet and pushed him toward the door. "Go on, kid. Take him home."

I got on one side of him and Shard took the other. "Let's hope we can get him home without him kissing the sidewalk," she said.

That was the least of my troubles. I just wanted to get him back before Mrs. Family Services arrived with the cops. It was slow going. But I was relieved to see the coast was clear as we approached the front steps of our building, which is called Sunnyview Terrace — another name that was a joke. The old factories all around blocked out most of the sun, our view was of a Dumpster in an alley and the only "terrace" was the parking lot with weeds pushing their way through the cracked pavement.

"Lift your foot, Dad."

He stood in front of the stairs and stared at them blankly, as if he had never seen stairs before. "Up. Up!" Shard said, trying to show him how to bend his knee.

Dad seemed to notice her for the first time. "Who is she?" he said, loud enough for the guy standing at the bus stop just past the apartment building to turn and stare.

"It's Shard Kent, Dad. From down the hall." I tried to whisper so no one else would look.

He kept staring at her. "That's a stupid name," he said.

Shard's cheeks turned pink. I felt my stomach twist. Why did he have to say rude stuff like that? And besides, that was quite a statement, coming from someone named Dearing.

"It's a great name," I said, meaning it. "And we're lucky she's helping, seeing as you've forgotten how to lift your leg."

Shard gave me a small smile.

"I haven't forgotten anything . . . see?" My dad lifted his leg and held it there like a dog trying to pee on a fire hydrant.

"Just get up the stairs!" I said through clenched teeth. People were starting to stare from across the street now.

It took forever to get him up the steps, through the front door and then up the stairs inside to the second floor. We almost had to drag him down the hall, and I was never so relieved to open the apartment door. We pulled him inside and dumped him on his bed. He flopped on it face down as limp as cooked spaghetti, bounced once and started snoring.

I took off his shoes and covered him with the covers that weren't pinned under him. I left the door a bit ajar in case he took the fits tonight. Mom told me they were seizures from drinking. They were horrible to watch. Mom used to take care of Dad when he was like that, but now . . . well, I did it.

"Thanks for helping," I said, going back into the living room.

"No problem."

"You want to watch some TV?"

"Sure. Merle and Reese always hog it at our house. If I have to watch one more episode of *Bananas in Pyjamas*, I'm gonna put a foot through the screen."

I didn't doubt for a minute that she meant it. Shard has problems with her temper. All the Kents do. Sometimes the noises coming from their apartment sound like a herd of bison square dancing.

We sat together on the couch and turned on a ghost-hunting show. I hoped the investigators didn't find anything that would give me nightmares.

"By the way, sorry for what my dad said."

"About what?"

"About your name being stupid. It's not. He says dumb things when he drinks."

She shrugged as if she didn't care, but I could see by the way she chewed her lip that she did.

"You're lucky to have a name like that. I mean, who wouldn't want to be named after a jagged piece of glass?"

"I'm not."

"You're not lucky?"

"I'm not named after a jagged piece of glass."

"S-h-a-r-d. That's totally a jagged piece of glass."

"It's short for Shardonnay."

I'd spent enough time waiting for my dad in the wine aisle to know what Chardonnay was. "Chardonnay is spelled with a 'C,'" I said.

"My mom can't spell."

"So you're named after a kind of wine?"

"Mom said it was a private joke between her and Dad. Apparently I was born because of a bottle of Chardonnay."

Why do parents always screw up when naming their kids? Don't they know that name will follow them all their lives? Or at least until they are eighteen and can change it to something decent. But by then the damage is done — an entire childhood of trying to come up with a shortened version to deflect teasing, and worrying that your full name will be read out from the attendance sheet. Whenever Mrs. Morton in grade two read my name out, it sounded like Chris Dearie. I took a lot of ribbing for that.

"It's still a cool name," I said.

She gave another small smile. We watched the ghost investigators walk around in the dark with digital recorders looking for cold spots. In the end, all they got on tape was a faint noise they said sounded like "Get out!" but just sounded like static to me.

"I better get going," Shard said. "See you tomorrow."

I followed her to the door and locked and chained it after she'd gone. I rummaged in the kitchen and found an open box of saltines and some pickles. I sank onto the couch and changed the channel just as the pounding on the door started again.

CHAPTER 4
A WOLF AT THE DOOR

I sat, frozen to the spot. Was Mrs. Family Services back already? Did she bring the police with her?

The banging got louder and louder. It was stupid to just sit there because I couldn't pretend we weren't home — my dad was snoring so loud it sounded like a jackhammer ripping up floorboards. I got a kitchen chair and dragged it over to the door so I could look out the peephole.

It must be true that opposites attract because two people couldn't be more different than Mr. and Mrs. Critch. He is the size of a football linebacker and she is like a toothpick. If I were her, I'd be worried that a hug from him would snap my spine in two.

Despite the fact that he is at least three times as big as me, I have never been so relieved to see the landlord before. He was just looking for the rent, which of course we didn't have.

I moved the chair and cracked the door open, leaving the chain on. "Hello, Mr. Critch."

Mr. Critch grunted as a reply. "The rent is two months overdue."

"Oh, well, my dad's asleep right now . . ."

"You mean he's passed out." Mr. Critch put a hand on the door, making it clear he could probably snap the thin chain holding it closed with just a push. "Tell him when he wakes up that he's got twenty-four hours to get it to me. In full. Or you're out."

"I'll tell him."

I shut the door and leaned against it, breathing like I had just run a marathon. Two months? How did that happen? I thought Dad had paid last month. This was worse than I thought. My dad was too proud to accept welfare and if he did go to work, day labourers made minimum wage — it wouldn't even make a dent in two months' rent.

I pushed the chair back under our half-circle kitchen table and curled up on the couch. I felt the pricking of tears behind my eyes, which I ignored, and wondered what we were going to do when the landlord came back tomorrow looking for his money.

A knocking woke me. I didn't even know I had fallen asleep, but when I managed to open my eyes, it was dark outside. The news was on so I guessed it was after eleven. Dad was still snoring, but more softly now. Who would be at the door at this hour? It couldn't be the landlord yet, and Mrs. Family Services would have to be home asleep. The cops? Nah, they would pound with their fists.

The knocking started again. I dragged the kitchen chair back over to the door and had a look. There was a man standing on the other side. He looked kind of familiar but I couldn't place him. He knocked again.

I kept the chain on and unlocked the door. This time I thought of the tips Shard had given me about answering doors to strangers, and I opened it just a crack with my foot behind it so he couldn't jam it open and I could slam it shut in a second if I needed to.

"Yeah?" I said.

The man's face smoothed into a smile. "Hiya, kid. Just wondering if your dad and you made it home okay tonight."

Now I knew who he was. He was one of the guys at the table with my dad in the bar.

"Uh, yeah."

"Oh, good. Good. Well, your dad left his wallet in the bar and I thought I'd drop it off."

Every antenna in my body went on silent alarm. It *was* my dad's wallet but I'd dragged him out of enough bars to know that the kind of people who sat with him don't return wallets to guys who are too drunk to remember leaving them behind. Every one would have kept the money and tossed the wallet in the garbage. Even Fiona. This smelled worse than the Dumpster on garbage day.

"Gee, that's really nice of you," I said, trying not to sound like I was onto him. "How did you know where we lived?"

"Fiona told me."

That sounded fishy. Fiona did know where we lived because she helped me get my dad home once when he had one of his fits right in the bar, but I couldn't really believe she would tell this guy. But then, Fiona was a bit of a mystery.

"Well, thanks a lot, uh . . ." I said, holding out my hand through the crack for the wallet, not knowing his name.

"Randy."

"Right, Randy," I said. I wondered if he knew his name meant "Wolf." A wolf at the door . . . that couldn't be good. "I'll give it to him."

"I'd rather give it to your father personally. Can I come in?" he asked, pulling the wallet out of reach and pasting a fake smile on his face again.

Shard would take a strip off me if she knew I was even thinking of letting him in. But I was torn. If there was *any* money left in the wallet, it might at least buy us a bit of time with Mr. Critch. And it was also plain that Randy wasn't going to pass the wallet in through the door. Maybe I could wake my dad long enough to get his wallet and get rid of this guy.

"Just a sec." I closed the door and ran into the bedroom. Dad was lying on his stomach, his head turned to the side, his mouth hanging open, his breath stinking of booze. It was the same position he had landed in hours ago when we dumped him there. I shook him. Hard. The snoring stopped briefly and he grunted and tried to open his eyes.

"Dad. Dad! Wake up."

"Mmmmph," came the reply.

Well, that was a waste of time. I knew it was a bad idea, but we needed the money. I went back to the door, undid the chain, swung the door open and let Randy in.

"Thanks, kid," he said as he went to the bedroom.

I didn't like this at all. I followed him in. "He's still sleeping, but I'll take his wallet," I said, holding out my hand.

Randy gave me a lopsided grin. "Yeah, sure.

Here you go." He tossed the wallet so that I had to use two hands to catch it.

I opened it to check for cash. There was a fifty inside. I got a sick feeling when I saw it. The money my dad had taken from the tea tin was all in twenties. Someone else had put this money in here.

When Randy's back was turned, I slipped the fifty into the waistband of my underwear, in case he changed his mind and snatched the wallet back. Then I set the empty wallet on top of the TV.

Now all I had to do was get this guy out of here, but he didn't seem in much of a hurry to leave. He was leafing through some of the letters on top of the dresser. What was this guy looking for, anyway? And what gave him the right to paw through our things?

"That's my dad's stuff," I said, trying not to let my anger show and talking really loud, wishing Dad would at least move on the bed. Randy was twice my size and his muscles bulged like ropes on his arms.

"Oh, sorry," Randy said.

He dropped the letter, gave a lopsided grin again and ambled out into the kitchen and headed for the fridge. He opened it and pulled out the half-empty jar of pickles. He twisted off the lid and put his grimy hand right into the jar to pull one out. I was seriously grossed out. No way I could eat the few that were left after his filthy fingers had been in there. He sat down on the creaky chair and crunched, pickle juice dripping onto the floor. I stood by, unsure of what to do. I wished desperately that my dad would wake up. When he went to work, he spent his time doing heavy lifting, digging and hauling. Even drunk, I'm sure my dad could still get this guy to leave.

"So, it's just you and your old man?" Randy asked, taking another bite. "Where's your mom?"

I hesitated before answering. Who was this guy to be digging around in our business, anyway? Sitting there like he owned the place.

"She's away. She'll be back soon."

Another grin. Another bite. Then, "Maybe she's up in the Yukon working the family gold mine?"

Are you kidding me, I thought. *What family gold mine?* Don't tell me this guy believed my dad's wild drunken tales from this afternoon.

"There's no family gold mine. My dad makes up stories when he's drunk."

Randy set the pickle jar down on the table. "Sounded to me like it was for real. Knew directions, coordinates, everything."

"I'm telling you, it's all made up," I said. "He doesn't know what he's talking about when he drinks!"

Randy looked around. "Then what's that?"

He pointed to a black-and-white photo hanging on the wall over the TV. It was a picture that had been hanging there for years.

"That's just my granddad."

"Looks like he's holding a pan."

"A pan?" I looked closer at the photo that I'd seen my whole life. My granddad was squatting down near some water wearing a long-sleeved shirt, jeans and a wide-brimmed hat. He had a full black beard and in his mud-caked hands was a flat metal pan partly filled with water. "So?"

"Don't you know anything? That's for panning gold." Randy shook his head at me. "I think I'll just have a little look around, okay?"

NO! I yelled in my mind. *It's not okay.* But outside I was quiet. Randy's smile was gone and I was smart enough to know when I was out of my league. This guy could knot me up like a pretzel without breaking a sweat. I decided for my personal safety to take the innocent route. "What are you looking for? Maybe I can help you."

"Where's your dad keep his important papers?"

"Like what?"

"Oh, I dunno. Maps, deeds, certificates."

I snort-laughed. "Deeds? Do we look like we own property?" I spread my hands out to indicate the cramped five-room space we called home: two tiny bedrooms, a bathroom, a galley kitchen and a living room.

He grunted at that, went through all the kitchen cupboards and then moved to look behind the TV and under the couch cushions. I stood helpless, watching him. I hated that feeling.

"Look, whatever it is you're looking for, we ain't got it," I said, trying again.

I had to get rid of this guy. Randy headed toward the kitchen again, probably to finish off the pickles. As he walked by, he snatched the old black-and-white photo of my granddad off the wall. He sat down at the kitchen table and turned it over. There was writing on the cardboard backing: *Wallace Dearing, Cottonwood Creek.*

He grinned. "Not a real story, huh?" He flung the picture at me and I caught it just before it landed on the floor and the glass smashed into a thousand pieces.

"Who. Are. You?!" a voice rasped. My dad, red-eyed and with two day's growth of beard, stood in the doorway to the kitchen. Both hands held on to the door jamb as he swayed gently back and forth.

"I'm Randy. From the bar," he said, getting up and extending a hand.

"What bar?" my dad asked, ignoring his hand.

"The Bull and Brambles. You were there this afternoon."

My dad stared and said nothing. It was hard to tell if he was trying to remember where he had been that afternoon, or whether he was actually asleep, standing up with his eyes open.

"I, uh, brought your wallet back," Randy said, pointing to the black leather billfold sitting on top of the TV.

Dad left the safety of the door jamb and shuffled closer to the table.

"Get. Out."

Randy opened his mouth as if he was going to say something, but then saw the look on my dad's face darken. He closed his mouth and went to the door.

"Thanks again, kid," he said with a smirk. I guess he had everything he needed.

When he was out I locked the door and pulled the chain across. Dad staggered back to bed. I collapsed on the couch.

CHAPTER 5

THE MAN WHO LOST EVERYTHING

The sunlight pierced my eyelids and forced me awake. For a brief moment I let myself believe that Mom was in the kitchen and any second I would feel the touch of her hand gently on my shoulder to nudge me and tell me she was making chocolate chip pancakes for breakfast. The moment passed as the emptiness in the apartment settled on me like a fog, pressing on my chest.

I forced myself up from the couch, still in my clothes from the day before, and shuffled to the kitchen for a drink. Granddad's picture was still on the table.

I picked it up and studied it. Funny, but I had never noticed the pan in his hands before, and I had been staring at that picture forever. To me it always just looked like he was washing dishes in a creek or something. Who knew what those pioneer types did before dishwashers and plumbing.

"Fool."

I spun around. My dad was standing in the doorway. I was so focused on the picture that I hadn't heard him come into the room.

"Who? Granddad?"

Dad just grunted and went to the cupboard.

"Why was he a fool?"

Dad didn't answer.

I stared at the picture again. "Is it because he wasn't a very good prospector? I mean, if he had a rich gold mine, and was a good prospector, he wouldn't have died so poor, right?"

Dad dumped something out of a mug from the cupboard — I didn't want to know what it was — and spooned in some coffee crystals.

"No," Dad said, "he found gold."

"He did? Then what happened?" I asked. Knowing our family, there was a good chance he just drank all the money away.

Dad filled a dented pot with some water and put it on a burner. "He was told that claim was worthless, but then one day he said he found a vein of gold as thick as his leg. It went on into the hillside as far as he could follow it. Wouldn't let anyone near it, not even me."

"So, Granddad got rich?"

"No," he said, adding sugar to the mug.

"Why not?"

"Because he was swindled out of his claim," Dad said, his voice getting hard.

Well, that seemed about right. Even when things were going well for a Dearing, disaster was just around the corner.

"Filthy rats got away with it too," he added.

"Who were the filthy rats?"

Dad poured the boiling water out of the pot and into his mug and stirred in silence. "The same filthy rats that are everywhere, just waiting to lie and cheat and leave you jobless and homeless," he said finally. Then he took the mug of coffee and went to the couch. "Same filthy rats that live around here."

I followed him, still clutching the photo. "Why didn't he tell someone: the police, the sheriff, the Mounties or whoever is in charge up there?"

"No use."

"No use?! It was his claim. It was his gold!" I was almost shaking I was so angry. "Why didn't he DO something? Why didn't he fight for what was his?" *Like you should have done with mom*, I added silently.

Dad stiffened. "Weren't nothing he could do."

I wanted to argue with him, but you heard about stuff like that happening. Something was stolen and the police were too busy or there wasn't enough evidence or they didn't believe you. In the end, the crooks got away with it. Speaking of crooks . . .

"That guy from the bar, Randy, was snooping around for papers or a deed or something when he was here last night."

"That creep from the bar who was in the kitchen helping himself to our food?"

I nodded.

Dad grinned. "Well, he didn't find it, now, did he?" He took the picture from me and undid some little clasps on the back. The cardboard lifted away and he pulled out a worn and tattered piece of paper. He unfolded it carefully. It looked like some official form. Inside that was a yellowed newspaper article. It fluttered to the ground, face up so the headline caught my eye.

GOLD! GOLD! GOLD!
Lucky Wally Dearing Strikes It Rich!
His bad luck turns good after failed attempt to back out of land claim deal.

I picked it up to read the rest of it.

Wallace Dearing walked into the Bank of British North America this week with $10,000 worth of gold *nuggets from his claim on Cottonwood Creek near Dawson. This is the same claim that Wally disputed with the North-West Mounted Police only a month ago. Mr. Dearing reported that two young men, Ben Odle and Jonah Stuckless, sold him the claim for $800 one night while he was intoxicated. They believed it was worthless. When he tried to get his money back, Dearing's case was denied and he was stuck with the claim. He says that he has since found a pay streak on the claim of untold riches. Ben Odle and Jonah Stuckless could not be reached for comment.*

"Filthy rats," I said.

"Exactly," my dad said.

"So what happened to the claim and all that gold?"

"After your granddad found the pay streak, Ben and Jonah went back to court and argued that it was all a joke and that they hadn't really sold him the claim. They produced registration papers proving that it was still theirs. Said your granddad's papers were forged. The judge sided with them and they took back the claim."

"I don't believe it!" I said. "How could the judge side with them? It's obvious what they were up to."

"Some say the judge was bribed."

We stared at the picture.

"So what happened then?" I asked.

"Grandma Emma took us to live in Dawson where she worked as a seamstress to pay the bills. Granddad leased a claim nearby and I helped him mine it, but it was a dud. When I was old enough, I left the north to find work farther south. That worked out well," he said sarcastically. "Your granddad never gave up though. He died in the Yukon, a gold pan in his hands, they said. I only went back once, and that was when he was dying."

"Did the filthy rats get rich on Granddad's gold?"

A small smile played at the corners of Dad's mouth. "Nope. They never found the pay streak, though they looked for the better part of sixty years."

"What happened to the claim?"

Dad leaned back in his chair and folded his arms. "My buddies up north told me that after Ben died, Jonah kept renewing the lease so that our family couldn't buy it back."

"Even though he didn't find the gold? Why would he do that?"

"Spite."

Dad picked up the picture again and studied it. "I always wanted to go back and look for that pay streak." He put the picture down and stared off into space. "He told me where it was, you know, on my last visit."

All this was a bit much for me to take in. The gold mine being real. The swindlers stealing Granddad's claim. Deathbed confessions. It was like I was reading a novel.

"Where was it?"

Dad just smiled. Then the smile left his mouth. "Well, it's a pipe dream anyway," he said, getting up. "You'd need a ton of equipment and that's not free. And I'm not sure that Granddad wasn't delirious when he told me about this vein of gold. Maybe the others didn't find any gold because it's not there."

He didn't sound convinced, though.

Then I remembered I hadn't told him the other bad news. "Oh, Dad? Uh, the landlord came around last night." I swallowed. "He says we need to have two month's rent today in full or he'll kick us out."

"Did he now? I'd like to see him try." Then he sighed. "Where's the money?"

"You took it."

Silence.

"Oh yeah." He paused. "Well, pass me my wallet."

I got it from on top of the TV and gave it to him. He opened it and frowned. "Nothin' left?"

I reached into my waistband and pulled out the fifty. "Just this."

Dad took the fifty and stared at it. "I don't remember having a fifty."

"You didn't. You took twenties out of the tea tin."

"Then where did this come from?"

"It was in the wallet when that guy, Randy, brought it back last night."

"Really," he said. "Is it fake?"

I hadn't thought of that. I waited nervously while Dad held it up to the light and rubbed it between his fingers.

"Well, is it real?" I asked, unable to wait anymore.

"Close enough." He handed it to me. "Hey, shouldn't you be in school?"

"It's Saturday."

"Right. Well, when crotchety Critch comes screeching, give him the fifty and tell him we'll have the rest in a day or so."

"He said we had to have it all, or he'd evict us . . ."

"He won't."

I didn't really want to face the landlord again. Especially with only fifty dollars.

"You won't be here to do it?" I asked, trying not to sound desperate.

"I'm gonna go get the rest."

I didn't like the sound of that. Where was he going to get that much money in one day?

I didn't have the guts to ask him though.

"Oh, and Dad? Someone else came around yesterday."

"What was it here? A revolving door?" He took the last gulp of coffee and took the cup to the kitchen.

"Family Services came 'round. The lady wanted to talk to you. She said the school board sent her."

"You in trouble at school?"

"No. I mean, I've missed quite a few days . . ." I let the words trail off because I didn't want to lay a guilt trip on my dad by saying I missed all those days to take care of him.

"Then stop skipping classes."

He seemed to think that this would take care of the problem. He put his mug back in the kitchen, grabbed the empty wallet and went out the door. I didn't think it was that easy. Mrs. Family Services was not making a simple visit; she was bringing the police.

I wished I could close my eyes and when I opened them again this would have been all a bad dream. Mom would be coming into my room with a basket of clean, folded laundry while she hummed. She was always humming.

Humming can hide a lot of sadness. Most times I couldn't recognize the song, but it sounded nice. Dad would have steady work and we would have our own place, with no landlords threatening to evict us.

I knew it was stupid, but I closed my eyes, just in case. But when I opened them, all I saw was a rundown apartment, an empty tea tin and an old picture of a man who lost everything.

CHAPTER 6

UP FOR GRABS

I usually love Saturdays. If I hurry down to the Cornish Pasty bakery before it opens at eight, Alice will sometimes slip me some day-old sausage rolls out the back door for only a dollar a bag. And on the way back, I would share one with Bandit. He was the little stray that hung around our building Dumpster looking for food. Shard said he had some beagle in him. For weeks after I first saw him he wouldn't come near me, but now he sits patiently by the hole in the wire fence waiting for me. He knows what the rustling of the paper bag means.

But today I couldn't hang around and try and get him to come closer by holding the sausage roll in my outstretched hand. I had to leave it on the ground and sprint back to the apartment because I had the hateful chore of the rent payment hanging over my head. I did *not* want to have to face Mr. Critch again. He scared me. I'd never seen him smile the whole time we'd lived here. Not once. I was going to go crazy sitting here waiting for him to come around for the rent. And who knows what he was going to do when I told him we didn't have it all. Maybe he would rip my arms right out of their sockets. Or maybe hang me upside down by my toes from the ceiling. Or . . . I couldn't stand it.

I banged on Shard's door. Merle answered.

"Not in handcuffs yet?" she asked, looking hopeful.

"No. Get Shard, will ya?"

"Merlow Jane Kent!" I heard Mrs. Kent call. "Get in here and pick up these blocks. You near crippled me for life when I stepped on one. Reesling Marie, go and help her."

Shard came to the door and slipped out, closing it behind her. "Better get out of here fast. When Mom starts using full names, you know things are serious."

She headed back down the hall toward our apartment.

"Uh, no. I don't think we should hang out there."

"Why?"

"Because Mr. Critch will be coming around today for the rent . . ."

". . . which you don't have," she finished. "Been there."

"I'm supposed to give him fifty bucks and tell him to come back for the rest."

"No. No. No," she said, putting her hands up to stop me. "That's not how you do it. First we go back to your place and wait."

"Wait for what? For him to come and tear a strip off of me?"

"He won't come this morning; he does rent patrol around suppertime. Look, in about twenty minutes he'll head to the doughnut shop for a bagel and coffee. He does every Saturday morning. When we're sure he's gone, you slip down and give the money to mousy Mrs. Critch."

I breathed again. Leave it to Shard to figure out how to do what my dad asked and still keep all my bones intact.

I watched the sidewalk leading from the front doors toward the coffee shop from the balcony, while Shard watched TV. She seemed totally relaxed while I was a nervous wreck. Well, it wasn't her neck on the line, was it?

I was about to tell her that she was wrong when I saw him. Mr. Critch stomped down the sidewalk like he was on a mission.

"There he goes!"

"Well come on," Shard said, flicking off the TV. "Let's get this over with."

I was a bit embarrassed that I was relieved to have her along, but then Dearings never were very brave.

When we got to apartment 2B, I was ready to just slip the fifty under the door and run, but before I could, Shard thumped on the door.

"Whaddya want?" a voice asked as the door opened.

Really, Mrs. Critch looked even mousier standing there in her worn bathrobe with her hair hanging limp, but my heart was still pounding. Shard gave me a not-so-subtle shove in the back.

"This-is-part-of-our-rent-my-dad-will-have-the-rest-to-you-in-a-couple-of-days-goodbye." The words came out all in a rush. I didn't even wait for her to reply, I just turned and took off out the front doors with Shard on my heels. And I didn't slow down until I reached the corner of Dundas and Wellington.

Shard caught up to me, puffing. "What were we running from?"

"I just needed to burn off some energy," I lied.

"Uh huh." She didn't look like she believed me, but thankfully she didn't call me on it. "So where are we going?"

Where were we going? I sure didn't want to

go back to the apartment in case Mr. Critch took a fit at our measly partial-rent payment. What I really wanted was more information on my granddad and the claim in the Yukon.

"Where would you go to look up property registrations?" I asked.

Shard looked at me funny. "What property?"

So I told her about the claim and the gold and the swindlers.

"Filthy rats," she said.

"Exactly."

Shard thought for a moment.

"What you need is the internet. You guys still don't have a computer?" It was more a statement than a question; Shard knew we didn't have money for stuff like that. I shook my head.

"I'd let you use ours but Merle spilled fruit punch all over the keyboard last week and it's still not working."

"Where can we find a free computer and internet?" I said, almost to myself.

"The library," Shard said, sounding a bit exasperated. "Everyone knows that."

Sometimes Shard was a bit of a know-it-all. I said nothing because I didn't want to admit to her that I hadn't been through the doors of a public library since we moved here. Back when we lived in the row house on Hester Street, Dad would take me to the library on Saturdays while he checked the want ads. But now, Dad wasn't often in a reading mood. Luckily, Shard was already heading off. All I had to do was follow her.

The library really surprised me. I thought it would be like the one near Hester Street, which was housed in a red brick building with huge columns out front. That one had old carved wooden shelves and a librarian with a bun and reading glasses shushing me for coughing. This library had one whole wall that was all glass. There were deep armchairs where people were reading and a huge oval table with ten computer stations around it. People were chatting and keys were clicking and the whole place looked more like a lounge in a hotel than a library.

I turned to ask Shard where I should start, but she was gone — probably looking for a "Do-It-Yourself Martial Arts Training" book or something. I looked around for help and saw a sign reading *Research Librarian* on a small table. The woman behind it was young and pretty — she couldn't be a librarian, could she? A button on her sweater read, *Ask me! I'm Helen*.

"Um, I need some help finding information," I said, keeping my voice low so no one would notice that I had no idea where to go or what to do.

Ask-me-I'm-Helen smiled. "Then you've come

to the right place. What sort of information were you looking for?"

So I explained that I wanted to learn about gold claims in the Yukon.

"The books we have on the gold rush in the Yukon are fairly general, or were you looking for specific information?"

"Um, some general information and some specific." Did that sound as dumb to her as it did to me when I said it? She would probably boot me out now.

She punched some keys on her keyboard. "I've reserved one of the computers for you. Let's see what we can find."

She showed me how to find claim registration sites and even digital copies of old newspapers. I stared at pictures of hundreds of men, dressed just like my granddad in the old picture, standing on a pier waiting for a ferry to take them up the Yukon River to mine. Every one of them had a dream to strike it rich. I wondered how many of them saw it come true? Not many, by the sounds of it. Could my granddad really have been one of the lucky ones to actually find gold on his claim?

I switched over to the official site that had a document on how to register a claim, soil reports, maps with circles showing land heights all over them and fees. Then I opened another file with pages and pages of lot descriptions, their status and previous owners. One entry made my breath catch in my chest and my hands tremble a bit as I read on. Could what I just read be true?

"You ready to go? I gotta get home," Shard said suddenly, over my shoulder.

"Look at this!" I said, pointing to the screen.

Shard read the section. "Is that what I think it is?"

I nodded. "I gotta tell my dad."

We sprinted back, only slowing down when Sunnyview Terrace came into sight.

"Do you think Mr. Critch will be there?" I asked, getting nervous again.

"I think you're okay with crabby Critch for a while."

I relaxed.

"It's Mrs. Family Services you have to worry about."

Great. My stomach twisted into knots again.

CHAPTER 7

DON'T LOOK BACK

Shard jogged to her apartment. I stopped outside our door and put my ear to it. I was listening for voices. Cop voices. Family Services voices. Anything suspicious. But it was quiet inside. I decided I would have to take a chance because I was starving and saltines were better than nothing.

I put my key in the lock and turned it slowly. Were the police and Family Services waiting inside to grab me? I let the door swing open and stepped nervously inside. The apartment was dark and quiet. Then I heard a rustling from my dad's bedroom. I crept over to it and pushed open the door that was slightly ajar.

My dad was sitting on the edge of the bed, his head in his hands.

"Dad?" He looked up. His eyes were rimmed red and his hands trembled. I sat down beside him. "I've got great news."

Dad shook his head. "I've got news too."

Whatever his news was, it didn't look like good news. I guess he couldn't get his hands on the rent money. But my news would fix all that, I was sure of it.

"I did some research at the library. I looked up Granddad's claim on this government website."

"I want you to leave, Chris."

He wasn't listening to me. He was probably trying to tell me that we were being evicted, but that didn't matter anymore. We didn't need this crummy apartment.

"You know what it says? It says the claim is back up for grabs," I tried again.

"Get your things together. You don't have much time," he said.

"Listen! We can go up there and you can register the claim and mine it. But we've got to hurry. The anniversary date is in one week and if we don't claim it, sure as shooting someone else will."

"Go to the Kents'."

I jumped up, totally frustrated. "Dad! What are you talking about? Didn't you hear what I said?"

He looked up at me. "Yeah, I heard you. And believe me when I say I wish more than anything . . . if you had told me this on any other day, we'd be packing now. Why do you think I've kept that signed registration form all this time? I wish we could, I really do . . . but we can't."

He looked like a defeated man and I realized that his red eyes weren't from drinking, but from crying.

"What do you mean we can't? All we have to do is go up there, stick these notices to a post or a tree or something and then get to the registrar's office and give them the paperwork. And then it's ours, Dad. Just like that."

"It's never just like that." Dad snapped his fingers. "Not for me, anyway." His head hung down again.

I got a feeling in my gut that this was about more than being evicted from our apartment. "What's going on?"

Dad took a deep breath. "I'm about to be arrested and I don't want you here when it happens. So go."

"What? Why?"

"Well, let's just say my attempt to get the rest of the rent money didn't work out the way I'd planned."

"What did you do?"

"I was desperate and this guy I used to know said he would pay me a pile of money to drive a truck from the docks to another city."

"So?"

"If someone wants to pay you a pile of money and won't tell you what's in the back of the truck, take my advice: don't do it."

"What happened?"

"I didn't get far. Whatever was going on, the cops were already on the lookout because they pulled me over."

"What did they say?"

"I didn't stick around to find out. I took off on foot, but they got a good look at me and it's just a matter of time before they hunt me down."

"Are you sure?"

"Yeah. In fact, I think they're going to be here soon."

We sat in silence for a moment.

"What will happen to me?"

"If you're on Family Services' radar, they're probably going to want to take you."

"I'm not going into foster care. I'm not!"

Dad hung his head. "I don't really want you in the system either, but maybe it's for the best. You'll have decent meals and a place to sleep. I haven't done the best job since Mom left, and someday I'm going to make this up to you, I promise. But right now you have to get your stuff together and get out of here."

"I'm not going into care and there's no way you can make me."

"Chris, think about it. Where will you go?"

I didn't even have to think about it — "North. I'm going north to the Yukon and I'm going to stake that claim. And when you get out of jail, you're coming up there and you're going to mine the claim." I didn't ask if that was all right with him or if he thought it was a good idea — he had run out of ideas long ago. It was the only chance we had. Staying here wasn't an option.

Dad looked at me with a funny look on his face. "But you're too young. They won't let you register it."

I was glad that he wasn't questioning whether or not I was going or whether or not I would stake the claim, just that I might have some trouble because of my age.

"I'll figure something out. I always do, don't I?"

"And what about right now? Critch won't let you stay here, you know. He's serving his eviction notice tonight."

"I don't know. But I'll leave word with the Kents so you can find me."

Dad suddenly looked worried. He opened his mouth to say something just as we both heard it: footsteps coming down the hallway. And not ordinary footsteps — these were hard, clunky footsteps like cops' boots. And in between stomps were the clickety-clicks of high heels. No one in this apartment building wears either of those. The old folks who make up most of the tenants all wear non-slip rubber walking shoes and they move pretty slow. Everyone else wears running shoes, which make only a squeak now and then.

Time was up.

I raced to my bedroom and threw some clothes into my backpack. I grabbed Granddad's picture off the wall, wrapped it inside a sweater and shoved it in.

I ran to the kitchen and pulled my emergency exit out from under the sink. It was one of those fitness skipping ropes that sound like a great idea when you're watching the shopping channel at three in the morning, but that someone threw in the Dumpster. Probably when they tried it for the first time and realized the super-strength nylon could slice their shin if they didn't jump in time. I used this whenever I had to make a quick exit out of the apartment and couldn't use the door. Like when I was home alone and Mr. Critch came for non-existent rent money.

Then the pounding started.

"Mr. Dearing? Open the door, it's the police."

Dad threw me a hunted look. I ran to him and gave him a hug. We didn't say anything.

I hurried to the sliding door, opened it and stepped onto the balcony. I tied the skipping rope to the bottom of the railing and slipped on my backpack.

"Mr. Dearing!"

"I'm coming," Dad called, looking at me and buying me some time.

I climbed over the railing, still hanging on to the skipping rope, and let it dangle down. A skipping rope isn't the best thing to use for climbing because it's slippery and sways, but it got me close enough to the ground that I could jump down and not break anything. Once I was on the ground, I took off for the hole in the chain-link fence behind the Dumpster that leads to the alley. I didn't look back.

CHAPTER 8

FRIENDS IN LOW PLACES

I only slowed down when I was at the end of the alley and was sure no one was following me. I was safe, for now. But I had a bigger problem. Well, two bigger problems: Where was I going? I had nowhere to stay tonight. And then, how was I going to get to the Yukon? There was no way I was going to fail at this. To fail meant the end of the line for me and my dad. And as messed up as he was, he was all I had left of my family. We needed a new start and even though it sounds dumb, it was like my granddad was pointing the way.

So, where could I go? Not the Kents' — it was the first place Family Services would look once anyone mentioned that Shard and I were friends. I didn't really have any other close friends. The other guys in my class were friendly when we first moved here, but they stopped hanging around with me when they learned where I lived. Sunnyview Terrace wasn't in the best part of town.

There was only one other person who might help me out — Fiona. Yes, I know she owns a pretty seedy bar and has a temper, but she'd been pretty decent to me when my dad had a seizure that night in her bar and she helped me bring him home. Maybe she'd be decent again now. Or maybe she'd turn me in to Family Services. It was a crapshoot, but she was the only person I could think of.

I decided to go in the side door that opens into the alley. I was so paranoid about being nabbed that I worried Family Services would think to ask around the bars where my dad hung out and people would remember seeing me if I went in the front door.

I happened to know that the side door opens into the backroom where they keep supplies and wash dishes and stuff because that's the way we took my dad out that night. It's mostly kept locked, but I hoped someone was back there and would hear me pounding.

I had to knock three times before I heard the clunk of the lock turning.

It was Fiona who stared back at me. She propped the door open with her foot.

"He's not here, kid."

"Yeah, I know."

"So what are you still standing here for?" She had a really gruff voice when she was annoyed. I think I was annoying her. It made it hard to ask for a bed for the night.

"Can I come inside?" I was really worried that even in the dark alley, some busybody walking by would get suspicious.

She let out a big sigh but moved to one side to let me slip by.

"Well?" she asked once the door closed.

"Well, I, uh, wondered if you needed some help? You know, wiping down tables and stuff?" Yeah, I chickened out of asking for a place to stay. If you were standing there with her glaring at you, you would chicken out too.

"Do those tables look like they've ever been wiped down?"

It was true. The tops of the tables were sticky from spilled beer and other stuff that I didn't want to guess what it was.

"I could sweep up."

Fiona crossed her arms. "This ain't no employment agency. I got all the help I need. Now scram."

There was nothing for it, I had to come out with what I really wanted. "I really need a place to stay tonight."

"This ain't no hotel, either."

"It's just for one night," I said. I hoped she didn't ask why. I didn't want to tell her what was going on because she might not let me stay if she knew that the Department of Family Services was after me. Most people don't want to get involved with that mess. "I'll work to pay for staying. And I'm tough. I don't need a bed; I'll sleep on some chairs or something."

"Where's your dad?"

Now what was I going to say? I didn't want to lie, so a half-truth/half-lie was in order.

"He's with the police." Which was basically true, only he wasn't down at the police station — the cop was probably still standing in our apartment.

"So go home."

"Can't."

I held my breath, worried that Fiona would ask why I couldn't go home. I had no idea what lie to make up for that one. But maybe she'd had her own troubles with the law because she didn't ask me.

"Go to a friend's house then."

I looked down at my feet. That wasn't an option. Not only wasn't it safe, but Shard's family already had six people crammed into two bedrooms. "No room."

Fiona didn't say anything for so long that I finally got the nerve to look up again. She was staring at me with a strange look on her face. She grunted and jerked her head in the direction of the sink. "There's a stack of glasses needs washing," she said.

She didn't exactly say I could stay, but she didn't say I couldn't, either, so I headed to the sink, breathing again. I hung my hoodie on a nail in the wall by the door and got to work. Fiona went back out to the bar.

I didn't know time could crawl by so slowly. As I washed, I thought about my dad and wondered what was happening. Was he locked up? Could he get out on bail? Was he okay? I didn't even know how I would find out. I certainly couldn't just waltz into the police station and ask . . . they probably had a direct line to Family Services.

I would worry about it tomorrow. Right now there seemed to be no end to the glasses. Wash, rinse, dry, stack, repeat. My muscles weren't used to this and the adrenalin from my escape was wearing off. My hand shook a little and the glass in it started to slip, but I caught it before it crashed to the floor. I took a couple of deep breaths as Fiona brought in a whole new tray.

"So, is your dishwasher sick?" I asked, dumping the next load into the water.

"Nope."

"So, who normally does this?"

"Bar staff in between orders. *They* think this is great because they can serve more customers and make more tips." The way she said it made it plain that *she* didn't think paying another person was such a good idea. She also still hadn't said whether or not I could stay, but I knew from the look on her face that now wasn't the time to ask.

As the night wore on, the noise in the bar got louder and louder. I tried not to think about how hungry I was or when I last ate, but just as one of the waitresses, named Lisa, was setting down another load of glasses, my stomach grumbled.

Next time she came back, she brought a bowl of pretzels with her and winked as she put it on the counter.

I know pretzels aren't much of a supper, but when you're as hungry as I was, they taste like heaven. I tried to make the bowl last as long as possible. I would take a couple between washing and drying and lick the salt off before biting into them. I made that little bowl last through an entire tray. When Monica brought more glasses, there was a cup of peanuts tucked in among the dirty dishes. Sarah brought me a few nacho chips.

At last the flood of cups trickled to a stop. I looked at the clock on the wall behind me; it read two a.m. With the last tray, Lisa plunked a plastic cup with money in it down beside me.

"What's this?" I asked.

"We chipped in some of our tips for you. Figured we owed you, seeing as we were able to serve more customers, and more quickly, without having to stand back here up to our elbows in greasy water."

"Thanks." I didn't know what else to say. I hadn't expected this. When she left I dumped all the coins and bills into my jeans pocket without even counting them. Pictures of hamburgers floated in my mind. Tomorrow, I would feast on something greasy and hot. My mouth was starting to water at the thought of it.

"You done?" Fiona asked from the doorway. I was so tired I hadn't even heard her come in.

"Six more," I said. I stacked the last glasses and dried my hands.

Fiona headed to the back of the room and opened a door in the back wall. I knew she lived upstairs, so I was expecting to see a staircase, but this opened to a closet. I felt a chill go through me. She wasn't going to make me go in there, was she? I had this thing about small spaces — like old trunks in your cousin's attic that can be locked when you climb inside on a dare and you choke on the dust and think no one is coming back to let you out. A thing where my heart starts racing and I can't breathe. No way was I going in there. I would risk the streets first.

I tensed my muscles, ready to bolt at the first hint that that was what Fiona had in mind. Instead, she yanked on some metal contraption and pulled it out of the closet. It was some kind of folded-up bed with a thin mattress inside. She undid a metal clasp on the side and it opened up flat.

"I got this when Lisa was pregnant," she said, looking sort of embarrassed. "She said if she could lie down now and then, she could work up until her due date and I wouldn't have to find another waitress right away."

I didn't need an explanation; I was too relieved to know I didn't have to go in that tiny walls-closing-in-on-you, running-out-of-air closet.

"I'll be upstairs," she said, gesturing to another door, which must be the stairs. "I suppose you want a pillow and blanket?"

She phrased it like a question, but she left before I could answer. I didn't need anything. I told her already, I was tough.

She came back and set them on the mattress and then left again without saying another word.

Relieved and exhausted, I sat on the edge of the metal bed and took off my shoes. I didn't know how I was going to pull this gold claim registration off; I didn't even know how I was going to get up north. I took Granddad's picture out and stared at it, willing him to give me the answer. He just looked back at me with silent eyes. I turned the picture over. *Cottonwood Creek.* All those weird creek names up there: Cottonwood Creek, Deadman's Creek . . . wait, that was it! Granddad came through . . . I knew how I was going to get up north.

CHAPTER 9

THERE'S NOTHING UP THERE

When I woke up, I couldn't remember for a moment where I was. The stacks of cardboard boxes and trays of upside-down clean glasses brought it all back. So did my stiff muscles from bending over that sink so long last night.

The clock over the door into the bar read eight thirty. I hoped that was a.m. and not p.m. I was so tired last night, who knows how long I slept. The bit of daylight creeping in under the door-frame told me it was still morning.

Fiona was still sleeping. How did I know? I could hear her snoring all the way from upstairs. The walls were either as thin as paper, or Fiona snored louder than a running diesel engine.

Now that I was fully awake, my plan from last night on how to get to the Yukon seemed less brilliant than when it first came to me. I changed my shirt and socks with clean ones from my backpack and grabbed my hoodie, which was still hanging on the nail. I had to see Shard before doing anything today.

I slipped out the back door, trying not to let it squeak too much. The alley was quiet, but there was always the possibility of someone seeing me so I slid down it with my back to the wall. This was how a prison escapee must feel. I took as many back laneways as I could to get back to the apartment building. After crawling through the hole in the chain-link fence behind the Dumpster, I paused and caught my breath. I slowly stood up and peered out from the side of the smelly blue bin to see if anyone was hanging around waiting to grab me.

The parking lot was quiet and empty. Now, if the skipping rope was still tied to the balcony railing, I could shimmy back up and sneak through our empty apartment to Shard's place.

A whimper caught my attention. Bandit sat just out of reach with his head slightly tilted as if to ask where the paper bag was.

"Sorry, pal," I whispered. "No time for treats today."

Like a ninja, I scooted from car to car to get closer to the building without being seen. Then I sprinted to the spot under our balcony where I had left the skipping rope hanging yesterday.

Problem. The rope wasn't tied to the balcony railing anymore. Now how was I going to get in? I couldn't go in the front door — Mrs. Critch patrolled that from her front window. All I needed was for her to rat me out to Family Services. Or demand the rest of the rent. Neither thought appealed to me.

If I had a phone, I could just text Shard and tell her where to meet me, like normal people do. Except neither of us had one. Email was out too, because even if I did walk all the way to the library to use their computers to send one, her home computer was gummed up with Merle's fruit juice. This called for doing it old school.

I grabbed a handful of little rocks that were on the edge of the paved parking lot and headed around the corner of the building to where Shard's bedroom window was. I tossed the stones one by one so they made a tapping noise on the glass. All I could hope was that she was in her room and could hear it.

The face that popped up into the window wasn't Shard's; it was Reese's. I hoped she would get her sister and not call the cops "just for fun."

It was a relief to see Shard come to the window and for her to point toward the Dumpster. I ran back behind it and crouched down. This running from the law was exhausting. How do escapees do it? I think I'd turn myself in just to get some rest.

Shard came around the Dumpster. "Are you nuts?" She never did bother with small talk. She got right to the point. I think that was one of the things I liked best about her.

"No more than usual."

"Family Services has been prowling around here already today. They've been to our place twice asking if we've seen you."

I groaned. "Will Reese tell them she saw me?"

"I'll bribe her with something. Ten Jolly Rancher candies and a viewing of one of my 'kissing movies,' as she calls them, should cover it."

A "kissing movie" sounded like something I wanted to avoid, that's for sure.

"I need you to do me a favour," I said. Shard didn't say anything, but just raised her eyebrows. "I need you to go down to the police station and talk to my dad. The minute I walk through those doors, I'm as good as in foster care."

"So I go down there and say what to your dad?"

"Find out if he's okay, and tell him I'm staying with Fiona and that I have a plan to get north."

"A plan? Okay, let's hear it."

Now that I was going to have to say it out loud,

I felt nervous again. In my head it sounded possible. Out loud it was going to sound dumb.

"I'm going to ask Fiona to take me."

Shard snorted. "The Dragon Lady? Are you kidding? Why would *she* take you up north?"

"She buys that beer from the Yukon. Deadman's Creek, it's called. My dad loves the stuff . . ."

"Loves it a bit too much," Shard said under her breath.

". . . so she has to go up there from time to time, right? To buy it and stuff."

"She doesn't have to go all the way up there to buy it. All she has to do is pick up the phone or place an order online and they'll ship it."

"Oh." My shoulders sagged with the realization that, as usual, I was wrong. Now what was I going to do? "Well, that's that," I said. "I guess I should just turn myself in to Family Services, right?"

I was angry. All I could see was that I was going to end up like my father — no home, no hope. Another loser Dearing.

"Not so fast, Mr. Pessimist. Fiona doesn't need to go up there to buy beer, but she does go up there."

"She does? Why?"

"She's from up there, doofus. Didn't you know that? Don't you ever talk to people? Why do you think she even sells Yukon beer? Sheesh." Shard shook her head at me.

Hope surged back. I just tried not to think about how I was going to convince Fiona to take a trip home right now. But I would think of something.

"Will you go tell my dad, then?"

"Tell him what? You don't even know if Fiona will take you."

"She will. Just tell him, okay?"

Shard sighed. "All right. I'll do it. Meet me back here at one o'clock. But you owe me, big time."

Shard waited while I made my escape back through the hole in the fence and down the alley, in case someone tried to follow me. They'd have to go through her, and I don't recommend it. I mentioned her temper, right?

I headed back to the Bull and Brambles to talk to Fiona. This made my stomach churn more than meeting Mrs. Family Services. What if she wouldn't go? How else could I get up there? I didn't have enough money for the bus and there was no way I was going to try and hitchhike. Speaking of stomachs churning, mine felt like a pair of hands were grabbing it and twisting. I hadn't eaten anything since the bar snacks last night. I detoured into a fast food place and got a breakfast sandwich with some of the tip money from last night. It was greasy and hot and, best of all, stopped the ache.

I wiped my hands on my pants and took the lane that went behind the bar. I had one shot at this and I had better make it good.

There was a truck in the alley and a guy unloading boxes into the backroom. I slipped inside and saw Fiona counting a tower of boxes and checking things off on her clipboard.

"I need to talk to you," I said to her.

She stopped her scribbling and looked down at me. "Well sure. Just let me put all my work down. I'll let this delivery guy steal from me by not counting the order, and let him leave some boxes in the doorway so someone trips over them and then sues me for breaking their ankle, and I'll talk to you instead."

Wow. Talk about heavy on the sarcasm.

"Or . . . I can wait until you're done," I said.

Fiona made a sound that was a cross between a snort and huff and went back to her clipboard. I thought the best thing to do was lend a hand. The sooner the deliveryman left, the sooner I could talk to Fiona.

I looked at one of the boxes I was moving: *Old Dog Brewing Company.* And below that, *Deadman's Creek.* Was this a good sign or a bad omen?

When the delivery guy was gone, Fiona left to

go out into the bar. I followed her. I was running out of time.

"So, can we talk now?"

Fiona sighed. "I really don't have time for this."

"You don't even know what I'm going to say!"

"So far, every time you've talked to me, you've needed something."

Well, I couldn't argue that. Truth was, this was an even bigger favour. I had to ease into this.

"I was wondering how your family was."

Fiona stopped wiping down the bar and stared at me.

"My family?"

"Yeah. They live up north, right? You probably don't get to see them much."

Fiona stood absolutely still. "I see them as much as I ever want to."

"Oh." What do you say to that? Obviously not a close family. "I hear it's beautiful up there. You must miss it."

"It's cold eight months of the year," she said flatly.

Right. This wasn't going well. And Fiona was getting suspicious — I could see it in the way her eyebrows were going higher and higher.

"Oh," I said. *Just get to the point*, Shard would say right about now. "I was hoping you were planning on making a trip up north soon."

That statement just hung in the air like a half-filled balloon.

"No. I wasn't." She began filling little wooden bowls with pretzels.

Wasn't she even going to ask me why? Well, I would tell her anyway.

"I need to go to the Yukon."

She didn't answer. There was only the sound of glasses clinking as Fiona straightened them on the trays.

"It's really important. Life or death," I added. That should do it. The phrase "life or death" always gets results. She would have to say something now.

"Look, kid, I have a business to run right here and it's not a travel agency. You need to get up north? Take a bus." She went back to getting the bar ready for business later.

I was stumped. If "life or death" didn't get a reaction from her, what would?

"I don't have money for the bus." *Or the time*, I wanted to say. I had been doing some calculations. I would probably need nine or ten days to travel up there, find the claim, attach the tags and then race back to the office to register. From what I remembered looking at the map on the computer, the claim was a long way away from Dawson. I didn't even know how I would get there — borrow a bike? An ATV? Taxi? Did they even have taxis in Dawson?

I wished I'd had time to do more research at the library, but one thing I knew already . . . I had no time to waste. The anniversary date of the claim was now only six days away. After that, the first person to stake the claim got it. Every minute after midnight of that day that I wasn't up there was a chance to lose it.

"Not my problem," Fiona said.

"But . . ."

"Look, I put you up for the night. That's what you said, just one night. Now you need to get things figured out. I've got stuff to do."

She turned and went back into the backroom. I was stunned. I couldn't believe everything had fallen apart so quickly. What was I going to do now?

I sank down on one of the chairs and pulled out my granddad's picture. *I guess you were wrong,* I said to the face staring back at me. *This is a dead end. Another Dearing failure.*

"Where did you get that?"

I jumped at the sound of Fiona's voice. I hadn't heard her come back into the bar.

"It's mine."

Fiona snatched it out of my hands. "What are

you doing with Wally Dearing's picture?"

This was bizarre. How did she know his name? Or what he looked like?

"He's my granddad."

Fiona slowly raised her gaze from the picture to me. "You're a *Dearing*?"

"Yeah. My dad is Frank Dearing. He's in here all the time."

Fiona looked perturbed. "Yes, I know who your father is, but we're not exactly friends. And all he ever said was, 'call me Frank.' He never said his last name." She looked back down at the picture. "He's Frank *Dearing*?" She shook her head. Then her eyes narrowed. "Does this have something to do with why you want to go up there?"

I nodded. "I'm going to get my granddad's claim back."

"Wally's claim is back up for grabs?"

"You know about the claim?" I asked her.

"Everybody up there has heard about Wally's gold."

Why did the way she said that make my stomach lurch? I had a feeling that maybe I shouldn't have said anything about it. The fewer people who knew about this, the better.

"So, there are lots of people mining up there, I guess."

"Kid, everyone has a claim up there. Everyone's looking for gold."

"So, why'd you leave?"

Fiona took a deep breath and looked past me as if she were looking at something or someone else. "'Cause it's a hard place to make a living and I needed to eat."

Harder than here? I wondered. Because this wasn't exactly the land of riches, either. At least not for my dad and me.

"Getting a claim doesn't mean you'll make any money, you know," she said, looking at me again. "That's if you manage to get the claim. Most people fail to even repay their loans let alone make any money at it. It's a hard, cold, lonely life. There's really nothing up there for you."

"You're wrong."

Fiona and I were having a stare down. What did she know about whether there was something up there for me or not? My dad and I were sinking here, like we were caught in quicksand. The more we struggled, the deeper we went. Up there was a new beginning for us: Dad knew how to mine and would have ground to work. And I didn't dare tell anyone this, not even Shard, but part of me thought that way out there in the bush, we'd be too far from a bar handy enough for our money to be poured down my dad's throat. No one would know us. No one would whisper about my mother. No one would know my dad's record. We could start over.

Nothing up there for me? She couldn't be more wrong.

Fiona broke off staring first. She handed the picture back to me. I wrapped it up in a sweater and put it away.

I had to get back to the apartment to meet Shard. And figure out a way to get to the Yukon with no money.

I started for the door.

"Why can't someone else dump Uncle Joey in the river?" Fiona muttered to herself. "Like it's that hard. You find a quiet spot, put them in the water, they float for a while and then the current takes them away."

I froze. Did I just hear her plan someone's murder? Was she really going to dump a body in the river? Maybe it was a good thing she wasn't taking me north. Maybe I'd end up feeding the fishes too.

I put my hand on the knob and turned it quietly, hoping to make my escape.

"Wait a minute," she said, pointing at me. "This is your lucky day, 'cause it so happens that I *do* have to go north. I've been putting this chore off for months and this is as good a time as any. At any rate, it'll get my aunt Peggy off my back."

I started babbling. "You know, maybe I can save enough for a bus ticket after all. I mean, I don't want to put you out. It was too much to ask anyway."

You know how sometimes when you're trying really hard not to say something, and it's the first thing that pops out of your mouth? Yeah, that.

"I'm sure Uncle Joey won't mind if you waited." I smiled a nervous smile, wanting to kick myself for mentioning him.

"I doubt Uncle Joey will mind, seeing as he's dead. But I need to get this over with. It's been preying on my mind."

"He's dead?" What kind of family was this?

"Yeah. And in his will, Uncle Joey asked that I spread his ashes in the Yukon River by our favourite fishing spot. Don't ask me why Jackie or Aunt Peggy can't do it."

"Oh." Relief washed over me. But you really can't blame me for wondering. Fiona *is* strange.

"It'll take me a couple of days to get things in order," Fiona said.

"Sure. That'll be okay."

Actually, it made me nervous. Every day down here meant a tighter schedule up there, but this was no time to be picky. *Thank you, Uncle Joey*, I whispered to myself.

Fiona left me standing there and headed to the back again. I took a deep breath.

I was going to the Yukon.

CHAPTER 10

A HARD GOODBYE

"So, do you have superpowers or something?"
That was as close to a compliment as you get
from Shard. She couldn't believe Fiona had agreed
to take me up north. We were crouched behind
the Dumpster again. The aroma of rotting vegeta-
bles was starting to get stronger as the sun warmed
up the huge metal bin. We were going to have to
find a new meeting place soon, before I gagged.

"No. I just reasoned with her," I said.

"Puh-leeze. Now tell me what *really* happened."

I sighed. I hated when she was right. "She said
no at first, but then changed her mind."

"Why?"

"I dunno. She got real quiet when she saw
my granddad's picture. And then she remembered she had to dump Uncle Joey's ashes in
the river."

"Wait. She saw a picture of your granddad?

The one that hung on your wall? And she has to what?"

"I know it sounds crazy, but she got all weird when she saw it. Knew my granddad's name, all about the claim, everything."

"How did she see it?"

"I had it with me."

Shard crossed her arms. "That's the dumbest thing I've ever heard. Why would looking at a picture make her suddenly want to take a trip to dump someone's ashes?" She gave me a funny look. "Are you sure that's what happened?"

"I'm sure." I didn't blame her for questioning it. It didn't really make sense to me, either. But whatever would get me up there, I'd take it.

"Doesn't it worry you that so many people seem to know about this?"

"This what?"

"The claim. The gold. Seems to be on a lot of people's minds."

"A lot of people?"

"Well, it sounds like everyone up there knows, and now you've told Fiona and there was that guy Randy who was sniffing around your place. Aren't you worried there's going to be a run on it?"

Was I worried? That's all I could think of lately, which was another reason I wished Fiona didn't need a couple of days to get ready to go. What if, when I got up there, someone else had staked the claim already? My stomach was starting to churn again.

"Nobody wants a claim with no gold on it," I said, trying to convince myself as well as her.

"I thought you said your granddad found a pay streak?"

"That's what *he* said. Nobody else found more than a few flakes."

It was true. Why would there be a run on a claim where there was no proof gold was ever found? There wouldn't be, right?

"So, how is my dad doing?"

"He wasn't there."

"What?!"

"They've moved him to County."

This was not good news. This sounded like he was in even deeper trouble than I first thought.

"So he doesn't know I'm at Fiona's?"

"Sorry. I didn't know what else to do, and besides, thanks a lot . . . they were grilling me pretty good about you."

Just what I'd feared. They were hoping I'd come in to see my dad so they could grab me. "What did you say?"

"I said you weren't back at your apartment, and what was I, your babysitter?"

"Do you think they bought it?"

"Probably not. Those guys are suspicious."

We both went quiet and peeked out from opposite sides of the Dumpster, looking for cops.

"I don't think we should meet here anymore," she said.

I nodded but it was a strange feeling to know I couldn't go back to our apartment. Ever, probably.

I needed to go. It was too dangerous to stay here. "So, thanks for trying," I said.

"I didn't say I didn't learn anything," Shard said.

"Well?" Really, sometimes Shard could drive me crazy.

"He's been moved to County, but only because the station cells were full. Last night there was a big rally to protest the new bridge the city wants to build on the outskirts of town that will cut through some bald eagles' nesting areas. According to the news, it started peacefully but then someone threw an overripe mango at the police and it went downhill from there. Forty-two people were arrested. Jails are overflowing. Your dad's court date is in a couple of weeks and the desk sergeant I spoke to thinks he'll be out shortly after that."

I didn't let her see the liquid that was pooling

at the sides of my eyes. "Thanks for finding that out," I mumbled.

Shard winked. "No problem. But I guess I won't be seeing you for a while."

I was surprised that that hurt even more than not having a home anymore. Shard was my go-to person for information. Especially about people. She understood people so much better than me. But she was right. I had to scram.

"Just one more favour," I said.

Shard rolled her eyes. "What now?"

"Will you look after Bandit for me?"

"The stray? He doesn't like me."

"He just doesn't know you."

"Look, you have a way with dogs. I don't."

"Just feed him something when you can. He's so skinny."

Shard thought for a moment. "Well, it *would* get me out of eating my mom's meat loaf. Does he like dry, flavourless bricks of cooked meat?"

"When you're hungry enough, you'll eat anything."

"All right. I'll do it — but even one slobber on my face and I'm outta there."

"Thanks," I said, relieved. I didn't want him to think he was being abandoned. I knew how that felt.

I gave her a little wave as I jogged down the

lane. I decided it was crowded enough on the streets now to be safe travelling along Salisbury Street. It was quicker than trying to go down all the little streets and back lanes to get to the Bull and Brambles. As I walked, I got a creepy feeling. You know that feeling that someone is watching you? I looked quickly over my right shoulder and noticed a car driving slowly, keeping pace with me.

The hair on the back of my neck was standing straight up. What should I do? Run, or pretend I didn't notice anything? I opted to just keep walking. I turned onto Wellington Street, hoping the car would keep going straight and then I would know it was just my overactive imagination.

But the car turned down Wellington and was still driving super slow. Now my heart was pounding so hard that I was having trouble breathing. I chanced another look. The driver was a man wearing dark sunglasses. I scanned the area, looking for an escape. I needed to find somewhere to go where a car couldn't follow, preferably in a direction away from the bar. I didn't want to give my hideaway away. I looked for an alley, a backyard with low fences — something.

And then I saw it. Between two houses on Wellington was a fenced walkway that led to the schoolyard of St. Peter's Elementary. As I went past the opening, I turned suddenly and sprinted down the long pathway. I could hear a car accelerate on the road. If the driver knew the area as well as I did, he would know that a left on Beverly and another on Glamis would bring him to the front of the school. There was no way I could outrun him. So as I reached the end of the path, I looked back. The car was gone. I spun around and sprinted back down the path the way I had come. I stopped near the entrance and looked to see if the car was waiting anywhere. When I didn't see it, I dashed across the street, ran back up to Salisbury and slowed to a jog so I wouldn't be noticed.

I had trouble getting my breathing under control and imagined that everyone was staring at me. One block before the Bull and Brambles, I took a quick look around and then disappeared down a side street that connected with the laneway that led to the back door. I was almost home free.

As I turned onto the lane, I stopped dead in my tracks. By the back entrance to the Bull was a police car. I froze. Before I could turn and run, the back door opened and an officer came out. I looked around frantically for a place to hide. There was a small wooden shed just behind the Bull, but it was padlocked shut. With a pretty big lock, I might add. Why would there be such a large lock on a shed that looked like a strong wind would blow it over? Whatever the reason, there was no way to get inside.

There was no time to try and pry one of the boards off, so I just flattened myself on the wall farthest away from the door. Problem was, as the police car began to back out, he would see me. I timed it so that I went around the back corner of the shed just as the car came into view. Then as it backed to the right to point down the lane way, and could see that side of the shed, I slipped around the third corner to the wall closest to the bar. Feeling a little lightheaded from not breathing, I heard the car accelerate and leave.

I almost collapsed on the ground.

Did Fiona rat me out? Is that why the cops were here? Could I really trust her to take me up north without turning me in? There was only one way to find out. I went to the door and knocked.

Fiona opened it. "Can't you use the front door?" she asked.

That was a suspicious question. It made me wonder if she wanted me to use the front door so anyone watching the place could nab me. Only one problem with that — I hadn't told Fiona about Family Services yet. Unless that cop just did. I kept one foot in the door jamb so that I could bolt out the door if this got worse.

"Why were the cops here?"

"Courtesy call. There was a break-in at Sam's Electronics last night. Thieves escaped through the back lane here. They wanted to know if I'd seen or heard anything. Why?"

Sounded plausible. Or was I just gullible? I had to make a decision — was I going to trust Fiona or not? Because there wasn't much point in making plans to go north with her if I didn't. And really, I had to trust someone.

"Oh, did you? See anything, I mean?"

"No."

"I'll get to work, then." I pushed past her and went into the backroom. I assumed I'd be washing dishes again. Fiona didn't say anything about me not staying, so I put down my backpack, rolled up my sleeves and got to work.

This time, partway through the night, Fiona disappeared into her apartment and when she came back down she handed me a plate with a turkey sandwich on it. I was so hungry my hands were shaking as I picked it up. It was gone in under sixty seconds.

"You know someone named Randy?" Fiona asked me, coming into the backroom and rooting around for more coasters.

Yeah, I knew Randy, the wallet thief. "No. Why?"

"He's been asking 'bout you and your dad."

"Asking what?"

"Where you are. Where your dad is."

Fiona was watching me real close. I told her it was probably one of my dad's drunken friends.

She leaned in to say, "Kid, he's bad news."

A shiver went through me that I couldn't stop. "Nothing to me," I said, hoping I looked unconcerned. I didn't want to tell her how stupid I had been to open the door and let Randy into our apartment.

Fiona stared at me for a few seconds more, then went back out to the bar.

I didn't like this. Now Randy was sniffing around? I did my best to concentrate on the glasses, but the truth was, deep down, I was really, really worried.

CHAPTER 11

PICKLES, CHEESE AND PANTYHOSE

The next morning, Fiona was up early. I hoped that was a good sign. I hoped she was packing and doing whatever she needed to do to leave the bar for a few days. I found her on the phone in the main bar. She was rolling her eyes a lot and slammed the phone down when she was done.

"Everything okay?" I couldn't help asking. *Please don't let her say that she wasn't going to take me after all,* I silently prayed.

"Just dandy."

"Who was that on the phone?" Please don't say Family Services.

"My mother," she said and took a deep breath. "My family can't wait to see me. And Aunt Peggy is making cabbage rolls for the 'Throwing of the Ashes' party she is planning." She made a face.

"Doesn't it make you happy that they want to see you?"

"You don't know my family," she said, stomping to the backroom.

I didn't get that. I would love to have family, even distant relatives, wanting me to visit. Maybe when you have a great family like that, you take it for granted. Well, Fiona would have to sort it all out for herself. At least she didn't say anything about cancelling our trip, and I was hanging on to that. I just wish we didn't have to wait until tomorrow. What if I missed out on staking the claim by one day? I would never get over it.

I didn't know what to do with the rest of the day; walking outside wasn't safe and I couldn't go back to the apartment. Fiona was busy doing stuff that I couldn't help with and I didn't have anything to pack. That was the worst — not having anything to keep my mind from wandering and making me nervous. In desperation, I grabbed a cloth and started wiping down the tables.

I wondered if Dad missed me and if he understood why I couldn't go visit him. I didn't wonder whether my mom missed me or not. I had trained myself not to.

I jumped when someone started pounding

on the front door. The bar didn't open until one o'clock in the afternoon. Who would be trying to get in at eleven thirty in the morning?

Fiona was in the back and didn't hear the knocking, so I made my way cautiously to the door. It was hard to see through the frosted glass, but I could make out that it was someone short, so unless Family Services was hiring kids to do their dirty work, it should be safe to open the door.

"Took you long enough." It was Shard. She pushed past me, closed the door quickly behind her and peeked out through the frosted glass.

"What are you doing here?" I asked. Don't get me wrong, I was happy to see her, happier than I'd ever admit to her, but we had already said our goodbyes.

"You've got trouble."

Really? Did she think that was news? "Yeah, and?"

"I was just heading out this morning when I saw Mrs. Family Services talking to someone outside your apartment door."

Could it be my dad got released already? My heart started to thump wildly.

"Who was she talking to?"

"I don't know. Some big guy with a ponytail."

I felt a cold shiver run down my back. It wasn't

my dad and I wasn't happy about who I thought it had to be — Randy. So now he was not only asking about us at the bar, but casing out our apartment too.

"What were they saying?" I asked.

"I couldn't hear the whole thing, but I heard him mention the Bull and Brambles Pub, and then she thanked him for his help. I think she's going to check this place out. I don't think it's safe for you to stay here."

Tell me this wasn't happening.

"But Fiona said she wouldn't be ready to leave until tomorrow! What if Mrs. Family Services comes in here?" I could feel fresh waves of panic wash over me. Maybe this was going to be all over before it started.

"So tell Fiona you have to leave early because Family Services is hot on your trail."

"Um, I didn't exactly tell her that part."

"What part?"

"About Family Services wanting to find me."

Shard put her palm over her face. "Are you kidding me? You didn't tell her? Man, I wouldn't want to be in your shoes when she finds out."

"If Mrs. Family Services comes in here tonight, I'll be in foster care before I have to worry about that." I said miserably.

Shard punched me in the arm. "Good luck.

I'm outta here before they throw me in foster care too." She took a piece of paper out of her jeans pocket and handed it to me. "Our phone number. Just in case." She took another look out the window and slipped out the door.

I put the paper in my front pocket. I hoped I'd never have to use it. Right now I just had to worry about whether there was any chance I could convince Fiona to leave earlier than she planned. Like in half an hour.

Before I could even think of a story to get her to do that, she burst out of the backroom. Like Shard would say, I'm not really good at reading people, but even I could tell she was upset. Call me a chicken, but I wasn't going to ask her what was wrong this time. Unfortunately, she told me anyway.

"So now my mom wants me to bring stuff when I come."

"Stuff?"

"A jar of her favourite gourmet pickles, organic goat's milk soap, Gorgonzola cheese, queen-size ultra-sheer pantyhose and on and on. What am I? Her personal delivery service? Not to mention how long it's going to take me to run around town to get all that stuff." She shook her head and muttered.

"Why doesn't she just get it herself?"

"Everything's way more expensive up north, and some of it you can't get up there no matter how much money you have, like her gourmet pickles. So when the family heard I was coming, they started putting in their orders with my mom."

So much for leaving early. At this rate, we wouldn't be leaving for days. "I can do it for you."

Fiona whirled around. "What?"

"I can do it. Just give me a list of what you need and where to go and I'll pick it up. I think it's really important that we leave tomorrow."

"You're really anxious to get up there, aren't you?"

"Yup." I didn't want to tell her that right now I didn't care where I went, as long as I got out of town before Family Services caught up with me.

Fiona sighed. "Okay. Give me a minute to write it all down and find you some petty cash."

Which is how I found myself standing in the aisle in Juan Carlo's Jardiniere Market staring at a row of jarred pickles. I had never seen so many pickles in my life. The labels on them all had pictures of farms or grandmas in aprons, and fancy script announcing the wonderful pickle concoction inside: *Belly Buster Pickles, Just-Like-Grandma-Used-to-Make Pickles* and *Hot! Hot! Hot! Chili Pepper Pickles*. It took me forever to find

Fiona's mother's favourite, *Mabel's Pucker-Up Sour Garlic Pickles*. Only one item was crossed off my list and I had been gone forty minutes already.

I powered my way through the list. The worst one was getting the pantyhose. I had been standing in front of a huge rack of packages in the drugstore for what felt like an hour when an older lady came over to help me. I told her I was buying them for my mom who was sick and she looked at my list and plucked out a package in seconds. One taupe queen-size control-top sandalfoot pair of hose was finally in my hands. I thanked her, ran to the checkout, paid for them and got out of there like a swarm of bees was chasing me. I sure hoped this gold claim was worth public humiliation.

It was after supper before I was done. I grabbed a hot dog from one of those carts, silently thanking Lisa and the other bar waitresses for the tip jar that gave me some food money.

When I got back to the Bull, I chanced going through the front doors. The place was packed and there were so many people going in and out that I figured it was safe.

"So, how'd you make out?" Fiona asked me when I put the bags on the counter in the backroom.

"Got everything, I think. I couldn't find Mountain Gorgonzola, but the lady at C'est

Cheese told me the Gorgonzola Piccante is the same thing."

"Uh, sure," she said. "Thanks."

"So, are we still a 'go' for tomorrow?"

"Do you know a Mrs. Ledbetter?" Fiona asked, not answering my question.

"No."

"Are you sure?"

Mrs. Ledbetter? Who could that be? Uh oh. Was that the real name of Mrs. Family Services?

"Yup, I'm sure."

"Short, chunky lady with squinty eyes?"

I felt dread wash over me. It *was* Mrs. Family Services. I shook my head. "Who is she?"

"She came around here this afternoon looking for you. Said it was important. Said she heard you were staying here." Fiona was studying me carefully. I avoided her eyes.

"Never heard of her." Which was sort of true. I had never actually heard her name before.

"Huh. Well, she seemed pretty convinced that she knew you." Fiona turned her back to me and started unpacking the things I bought. "She gave me the willies, though. Reminded me of those vultures from Family Services that were harassing my mom when I was a girl. Always hovering around, waiting to snatch up some roadkill."

I stood completely still.

"I'm sure they mean well," she continued, still unpacking, "but they don't always know what's best for a kid." She turned around and looked right at me.

"Do they?" she asked me.

I slowly shook my head from side to side.

I might have imagined it, but I think Fiona almost smiled. "Looks like we've got everything we need, and Lisa is all set to take over the pub for a few days. So I think we'll get an early start in the morning. Don't want to be delayed by last-minute visitors or anything, do we?"

I shook my head again, still not daring to speak. I think if I did, I might cry. Guys named Dirk wouldn't cry, but I was still Chris and, sometimes, Chrises still felt tears well up behind their eyes.

I washed glasses until my fingers were wrinkly and my back ached, but I didn't mind. We were leaving for the Yukon in the morning.

CHAPTER 12
A SWEET RIDE

I dropped my backpack by the back door. I was all packed. It's not like it took me long. Fiona had let me, well, insisted really, that I use her shower this morning, so all I had to do was put in my dirty clothes and pull out clean ones. I double-checked that the registration paper signed by my dad was still tucked behind the cardboard, carefully rewrapped Granddad's picture so it wouldn't crack and, don't tell anyone, but I rubbed it for good luck. Stupid, I know, but I hoped at some point the Dearing bad luck might turn around and Dad and I would catch a break.

By eight thirty we were ready to go. I wasn't really sure how we were going to get there because as far as I knew, Fiona didn't own a car. Anytime I ever saw her outside the bar, she was walking. Maybe we were going to take the bus together?

But when Fiona came down from her apartment over the bar, she was carrying two helmets and wearing a black leather jacket with patches on the sleeves. I wanted to pinch myself — were we really going on a motorcycle? How cool was that? With her tough attitude and tattoos, I should have guessed that she was a biker. Stupid I never thought of it. The only downside was that the weather lately was damp and cloudy, and "cool" was going to have two meanings. Wind on the highways was strong and with only a hoodie, I was in for a cold trip.

"Where's your coat?" she asked me when I slung my backpack over my shoulders.

"Still in the apartment. It had a big rip in it and I didn't think I'd need it anymore this year."

Fiona gave this enormous sigh and went back upstairs. She came out with another leather jacket and handed it to me. It was pretty beat up, with darker areas where patches must have been removed. A few holes were worn through at the elbows.

"Looks like it's been run over by a truck," I said.

"Pretty much."

I tried it on. It was too big, but if I folded up the cuffs, it didn't look too ridiculous.

"Thanks," I said, meaning it. Big or not, it would cut the wind and keep me from freezing.

Fiona just grunted and I followed her out the back door into the lane.

"Hold these." She handed me the helmets and pulled keys attached to a long chain out of her jeans pocket. She went to the small wooden building behind the bar that looked like a garbage shed ready to fall down. A closer look, though, showed me the walls were reinforced with metal bars. Why would anyone do that to this crummy shed? I got my answer when Fiona opened it up.

Inside was a beaut of a bike. It was red and black, and on the side it had the word *Ducati*.

"I thought you'd have a Harley," I said. Isn't that what bikers rode?

"Do I look like an outlaw biker?" she asked. "This here is the sweetest ride your butt will ever have the honour of sitting on." She ran her hand over it like she was caressing it. "The Ducati Multistrada 1200 S. A Testastretta DVT engine with 160 brake horsepower and Skyhook suspension to make it seem like you're riding on a cloud. A fast cloud."

She backed it out of the shed and took her helmet from me. "Don't put so much as a scratch on it. Don't even breathe hard on it."

I snapped my helmet strap and carefully put a leg over, settling into the leather seat exactly the way she had told me to. There seemed to be no end to the list of instructions she had for me to be her passenger. Things like: not to bang her with my helmet, to lean with her around the turns, to dismount on the left only after she told me to and, most importantly, not to wiggle around because it would throw her off balance on the bike. The "not wiggling" would be the hardest.

We purred down the back lane and turned onto Salisbury Street. I realized then how handy the helmet would be. With it and the jacket, no one, not even Mrs. Family Services, would recognize me.

We wove our way through town until we came to a ramp and Fiona turned her head to tell me to *hang on*. My body tingled at the incredible surge of power as she accelerated and we sped along the highway that cut through town. It was the freest I could ever remember feeling, like nothing sad or miserable could catch up to me. The wind tore at my jacket and I was grateful I had it on.

After a while, the shopping malls and warehouses started to give way to open fields and forests. The endless waves of green flying by my visor looked strange and eerie. Even if the greys and blacks of the city reminded me of my dull and depressing life, I still missed the familiar surroundings. And every minute took me farther and farther away from my dad. Would he be all right without my help?

Although it didn't seem like we had gone that far since we left the Bull, I was already struggling to hold on to Fiona. I had barely slept in days, I hadn't eaten and despite the cool leather jacket, I was cold.

At one point Fiona glanced back at me and gave me a thumbs-up sign. I was afraid to let go to return the sign and was relieved when I heard the engine rev down and watched Fiona signal to turn off the highway. We pulled into a large gravel area packed with cars, bikes and semis, with a low building surrounded by empty fields.

I had been gripping the bike so hard that my knees buckled a little when I got off, and I couldn't wait to unsnap the helmet. It felt like it weighed a ton. I took a quick look to make sure there were no marks on the bike when Fiona wasn't looking. So far, so good.

Fiona had parked right in front of the low windows, and inside I could see tables jammed with people, heads down and digging into their food. I followed Fiona in the front door past a little room that looked like a miniature convenience store. The walls were crammed with stuff, from cold tablets and lighters to toothbrushes and big bottles of Pepto-Bismol.

The blast of heat inside the building revived me a bit. Fiona got us a table while I went to the washroom; that cold wind does things to your kidneys. I kept my hands under the hot water for a long time too, to get blood flowing again.

When I got to our booth, I had barely sat down with Fiona when a waitress plunked two platters down in front of us. Fiona must have ordered for me . . . and twenty other people, because there was no way I could eat all the food on that plate: three eggs, a pile of bacon, two sausages, a mound of fried potatoes and two orange slices. Then a waitress set a smaller plate with a mountain of toast down in the middle of the table.

"Thanks, Rose," Fiona said.

Our waitress smiled at her. "Any time, sweet-ie," she said, turning quickly and heading off, her rubber soles squeaking a bit on the floor.

"You come here a lot?" I asked, wondering how she knew Rose's name.

"A bit."

I should have known — I'd never get a straight answer from Fiona on anything. She kept pretty much to herself.

I dug into my breakfast. I wasn't used to eating

that much food at one time, but you know what? It was hot, greasy and delicious. I only left a few potatoes. I hoped the Ducati could handle a few more pounds on board. The real problem was I didn't have the money to spare to pay for it. If I had gone on my own, I probably would have survived on a bag of chips. I didn't want to spend any of my tip money because I had no idea how much I'd need once I got up north for forms and licences and things.

"Forget it," Fiona said when I began counting out dimes and quarters.

"Thanks," I mumbled. Who knows how much I was going to owe her by the time we got to the Yukon. I guess I'd have to skip lunch. And dinner.

"So how long will it take to get there?" I asked.

"Couple of days."

I couldn't go without eating for *that* long. And what about a place to sleep? We weren't even in a car where we could fold down the seats in a parking lot somewhere. I was starting to panic. Why was Fiona doing this? She was just a nice lady who wanted to help, right? I could trust her, couldn't I?

"Let's hit the road," she said, putting her jacket back on.

We wove our way through the tables. Suddenly

a bald guy with tree-trunk arms grabbed her by the elbow. "That yours?" he asked, jerking his head to where the Ducati sat outside the window.

"Could be," Fiona said.

The guy didn't say anything, but looked out the window again. With the chrome gleaming in the sun, the Ducati practically screamed *I'm expensive*, like a beacon for thieves. I braced for trouble, wondering if I could get out the doors before a chair was thrown at my head.

"Sweet ride," the guy said, showing a smile with a couple of teeth missing.

Fiona gave a little nod and continued walking. I jogged to keep up.

Outside, I did up my jacket, snapped on my helmet and climbed on. I could see several heads in the restaurant looking out the window. As we pulled out, there were even a couple of thumbs-up pointed in our direction. I was grinning as we got back up to speed. Living in a dumpy apartment and wearing clothes from those charity stores usually doesn't get you admiring looks. I felt on top of the world.

CHAPTER 13

PICK A NAME

Back on the highway, I concentrated on not falling off or freezing to death. I thought about my granddad, Wally Dearing, and everything that had happened to him. I got angry just thinking about how he was swindled. I could only imagine how he must have felt.

I started to notice that drivers were giving us the once-over as we passed them. This was a bike that got attention. All of a sudden, I realized that might not be such a great thing when you're trying to keep a low profile.

Then my worst nightmare came true. A cop car was coming up on our left.

For a second, it looked like he was going to speed on by, but then he slowed so he was level with us. I turned my head the other way, pretending to be fascinated by the cornfields. When I dared to peek over again, the cop car had dropped back slightly.

Oh man. My gut had a really bad feeling about this.

That's when I saw flashing lights reflected in my helmet visor.

Perfect.

Fiona signalled right and slowed down before we hit the gravel shoulder. All I could think was, *could I outrun the police? Could I hide out in the cornfield, maybe?*

I could hear the crunch of the gravel as the cop walked over to us.

"Licence and registration," he said.

Fiona reached into one of the side bags and pulled out a little black folder. The cop walked back to his cruiser, no doubt to run the licence number. I never thought to ask Fiona if she had any outstanding warrants. Was the trip over before we had barely begun?

More crunching gravel.

"Did you know your back right signal light is out?" the cop asked.

"No, officer, I didn't. I'll get that fixed as soon as I can."

The cop grunted and wrote something in his notepad. "And who's this?" the cop asked, indicating me.

Every muscle in my body froze.

"My nephew," Fiona answered smoothly.

I thought that I was a good liar, but Fiona was a pro. Even *I* believed her.

"What's your name, son?" The cop was looking at me now.

I flipped my visor up, then blurted out the first name that popped into my head. "Wally," I said. I guess my granddad's name came to me because I was just thinking about him. All I knew was, I couldn't use my own name. Family Services would haul me away before my feet hit the ground.

"Wally, what?"

"Marion," I said, without thinking.

"Spell it."

I swallowed hard. "M-a-r-r-i-e-n" I said, deliberately spelling it wrong so it sounded more like a last name.

The cop sauntered back to his car again. I started to sweat. Was he suspicious? Would it come back as a fake name? Or worse, was there a real Wally Marrien with a criminal record?

I tried to stop my hands from shaking. Being on the run was a scary business.

The cop came back and said nothing to Fiona for a minute. It was like he was trying to find a reason to hold her. Finally, he handed her licence back to her.

"Get that fixed within twenty-four hours," was all he said before he went back to his car.

"Will do," Fiona said, snapping her helmet strap again.

I pulled my visor down and tried to get my breath under control. That was too close for comfort. The cruiser pulled out and sped off.

Fiona turned around. "A fake name? Now you're lying to the police? What did you do that for?"

There was nothing for it; I had to tell her about Family Services. Fiona swore. Then she swore some more. She knew more swear words than my dad.

"And where did you come up with Marrien?" she said, practically yelling at me now. "That's the worst fake last name I've ever heard."

I shrugged. Fiona started the engine and pulled back into traffic, still swearing.

Marion was my mother's name.

CHAPTER 14

DOG WHISPERER

We had only been on the road a couple of hours and already we'd gotten too much interest from other hikers, the cops had stopped us and my fingers were starting to cramp where I was hanging on to Fiona's jacket. I didn't think I could feel my toes anymore. What a relief it was to feel the bike lean to the right and turn off onto a ramp.

It was weird, though. This ramp didn't have signs to a town, or even a truck stop. It was a road to nowhere but trees and swamps. Where was Fiona going?

We drove for a while down the road. Then, in a spot where the forest was creeping close to the pavement, she pulled off. A current of fear raced through me. She wasn't going to dump me here and take off, was she? When the bike came to a stop, I stayed on.

"Get off."

"Why?"

"Just get off. There's something wrong."

Was that some kind of a line? Didn't really matter, I guess. If Fiona wanted me off her bike, all she would have to do is grab me and lift me off. Reluctantly, I swung my leg over and stood on the gravel shoulder of the road.

"I knew that bulb shouldn't have been out. It was practically new." She pulled off the engine cover and started fiddling with the wires inside.

"What's wrong?" I asked. It wouldn't be good to be stranded out here in the middle of nowhere.

Fiona stood up and swore. I thought my dad was a big curser but Fiona had an extensive swear vocabulary. A word for every occasion, it seemed.

"My speedometer was acting up on the highway. I knew then that it had to be something electrical. Nothing I can fix." She looked up and down the lonely stretch of road. There wasn't a car or truck or bike to be seen. In fact, not even a building.

"I thought for sure this would take me to a town," she said, shaking her head. "Well, come on. There's got to be someone somewhere down this road."

We climbed back on. I actually couldn't wait

to get moving again. Here among the trees, with the sun high in the sky, it was getting a lot warmer. The breeze from moving would feel good. Fiona turned the key. The engine clicked. She tried again. *Click, click, click.* Nothing.

We got off again and Fiona pulled out her phone. "No reception. Of course not. Why would anything go right today?"

I didn't want to tell her that this was what my whole life was like. We stood for a while, listening for the sounds of an approaching vehicle, but there was only the buzz of some insect that sounded like a dentist's drill.

"Come on. There's got to be a house or farm or something down the road," Fiona said, releasing the kickstand and pushing the bike back onto the road.

"Are you really going to push that all the way?" I asked. It wasn't that heavy, but it looked uncomfortable the way she had to lean over to reach both handlebars.

"Well, there's no way I'm leaving a Ducati on the side of the road," she said.

I walked beside her. The swampy forest on either side of the road showed no sign of opening up into a field or pasture. There wasn't a hint that anyone lived down here.

"Want me to take a turn?" I asked, figuring she must be getting tired.

"No." She said it so quickly I knew not to bother asking again. Probably didn't want anyone touching her precious bike. So I stayed quiet. Another ten minutes of forest. Still no sign of life.

"Where's your mother?" Fiona asked.

The question seemed to come out of nowhere and it surprised me so much that I answered her. Normally I change the subject or go silent when someone asks me about my mom.

"She left to go help her sister. Out west, where she grew up."

Fiona said nothing. She just kept pushing the Ducati. The wheels made a crunchy noise as they rolled. "And?"

I sighed. I could have just ignored her, but there was something about being way out here with no noise, no traffic and no people that made me feel like, if I said anything here, it would stay private and locked away in the forest. It wouldn't, of course, because Fiona would know, but who would she tell?

"My aunt Irene had cancer," I said finally. "She never got married or anything. She lived with my grandparents until they died and then she lived alone in the farmhouse. So when she got sick, my mom said she needed to go out to take care of her sister."

"So how is she doing? Your aunt Irene, I mean."

"She died."

Fiona stopped pushing.

"Sorry to hear that. When?"

"A year and a half ago."

"Soooo . . . where's your mother now?"

The dentist drill insect noises were louder now. I took a deep breath. "She never came back."

I was glad Fiona didn't say anything. Nothing she said would have made things better anyway. I hated when people would make that *tsk*ing sound and pat you on the shoulder and tell you everything would work out. They were wrong.

I used to ask Dad when Mom was coming home, until one night when he yelled at me to stop asking, that she was never coming back because he was a "lousy drunk." I don't know if that's the real reason, or whether he was just saying that because he had been drinking that night, but that was the last time I mentioned her name — until today, when I told the policeman that "Marion" was my last name. I can't tell you why her name came to me just then.

We finally saw a farmhouse. It didn't look all

that inviting. In fact, there was a *Beware of Guard Dog* sign on a post at the road. Sure enough, as we turned up the lane, two dogs came barrelling toward us, ears flat and teeth glinting in the sun. We stopped dead in our tracks. No one came out of the rundown house or the weathered barn to stop them.

They skidded to a stop a dog bite away from us.

"Nice puppies," Fiona said with a quiver in her voice.

The dogs answered by barking even louder and angrier. Still no one appeared from the house. Fiona was rooted to the spot.

"Hey, boys," I said in a soothing voice. "You fellows are doing a good job." I slowly squatted lower to appear less threatening. "Good boys. It's okay. We're friendly."

I put out a fist and they came to sniff. Satisfied, they stood panting with their big fleshy tongues hanging out.

"How did you do that?" asked Fiona, still too terrified to move a muscle.

"I have a way with dogs," I said, feeling a quick clench of my heart as I thought of Bandit. Was Shard looking out for him?

I stood back up slowly, still talking in low, quiet tones. Fiona started backing down the lane to the road. The dogs watched us go, and when we were on the road they turned and loped back to the barn.

"What now?" I asked. It was the only house we had seen all afternoon. But Fiona wasn't paying attention to me; she was looking at her phone.

"Well, well, well. These people may have the meanest dogs in the world, but they also have cellphone reception." She touched the screen and held the phone up near her ear.

I could hear ringing, but no one picked up. She tried another number. Same thing. And another. Still no answer.

"Is no one working today?!" Fiona yelled in frustration.

Then we heard something wonderful — the sound of a running engine. In a moment, a pick-up truck came into view. We were saved! I was about to jump up and wave my arms, but before I could, Fiona grabbed my shoulder and whispered, "Don't do anything."

"Why? Isn't this what we've been waiting for?"

Fiona never took her eyes off the pickup that was coming closer. "I have a bad feeling about this," she said. "Put your helmet on. Quickly!"

My helmet? What was the point of putting

on a helmet when the bike wasn't running? But Fiona was clearly upset about something, so I did it.

As the pickup came beside us, I could see two guys inside. They were eyeing the Ducati pretty closely. I saw Fiona give them a friendly smile and wave and climb on the bike. I got on behind her. She pretended to dig around in her side bag, and I could see the guy in the passenger seat watch us until the pickup rounded the corner a ways down the road.

Fiona took her helmet off again. "We have to get out of here."

I took mine off too. "What was wrong? Why didn't you ask them to help us?"

Fiona started pressing the screen of her phone again. "I didn't like how slow they were driving and how they were salivating over the bike. If they knew we couldn't get it going, they might have grabbed it and thrown it in their truck."

I was getting a headache. So far, I didn't like life on the run. "Can I use the phone?" I asked. "I know who can help us."

Fiona shrugged and handed it over. I pulled a crumpled scrap of paper out of my jeans and dialled.

CHAPTER 15

THE MUFFIN MAN?

You know how guitar strings are stretched tight so that when you pluck them, they make a sound? That's how my nerves felt sitting there on the side of the road. Two hours crawls by when you are waiting for someone. I was ready to jump out of my skin at any sound. I was sure those guys in the pickup were coming back to get the bike, or that the crazy dogs from the farm down the road would suddenly decide to leave their yard and attack us, or that Family Services or the police would come screeching down to pick me up at any minute.

I don't know whether I was starting to sweat because of the tension or because the sun was getting high in the sky. I pulled off my jacket and had a closer look at it. The dark spot on the back from an old patch was an odd shape. It was pointy on the sides, as if the image had wings. Maybe some more butterflies, like Fiona's tattoos.

I knew all Fiona had on the back of her new jacket was a rectangular patch with the words *Well-Behaved Women Seldom Make History* on it. I knew because I had been staring at it the whole time we were riding. I guess Fiona didn't consider herself a "well-behaved woman." Come right down to it, I don't think my mother was either — leaving us like she did and never coming back. But I doubt she was going to make history, except maybe as a lousy mother.

I wondered how Fiona was not a well-behaved woman.

"What patch was on here?" I asked her, pointing to the dark spot on my jacket.

Fiona stared at it for a moment and then looked away. "Nothing."

"Well, it was *something*," I said, not letting up. After all, if she can make me talk about my mom, then she needed to come clean too. "Did it have wings? Was it your club?"

I'd seen enough biker jackets on guys in bars that I dragged my dad out of to know that's what was normally on the back of a leather jacket.

Fiona sighed. Not a sad sigh, more like an angry sigh that I wouldn't leave her alone. "Yeah."

"So what club was it?"

"Ladyhawks."

"Who are they?"

"You ask too many questions."

"Why didn't you put the patch on your new jacket?"

"I burned it." Fiona said this with a lot of bitterness in her voice.

"Oh." I thought that would have to be a big deal. People don't leave their biker clubs and burn patches just because they're having a bad day. Something must have happened. "Why?"

"Because *they* burned *me*," Fiona said, getting up and walking down the road and shading her eyes with her hand, indicating that the conversation was over. Except now I really wanted to know why she left her club. And did they burn her, like with fire, or burn her, like betray her? I didn't have a chance to ask because just then we heard the sound of an engine. There was a bend in the road, so we heard it before we could see it.

We both put on our helmets automatically, and I slipped on my jacket in case we had to pretend like we'd just stopped for a pee break or something and would be on our way. If it was the pickup truck again, they would know we were broken down and we'd be sitting ducks.

It wasn't the pickup. It was a white cube van that was coming straight for us. As it got closer

I could see that there was a big guy driving, and a shorter person in the passenger seat waving frantically.

Shard.

I can't even say how happy I was to see her. And I would never tell her, because she has a big enough head already.

"Is it your friend?" Fiona asked.

"Yup. But I don't know who's with her."

The truck was still rolling to a stop when the passenger door flew open and Shard hopped out. "Could you find a more remote place to break down?" she asked.

"No, we tried," I answered sarcastically.

"Seriously, it took us three tries to figure out what exit you took, and how far down you were—"

The man had gotten out of the driver's side and was coming over with his hand extended and a huge smile on his face. "Well, hello! So glad we found you."

He shook Fiona's hand as she stood gaping up at him. He was a full head and shoulders taller than her. "And you must be Chris," he said, coming to me next. He pumped my hand up and down so hard I thought he was going to dislocate my shoulder. His smile got wider the more he pumped. How can anyone be that happy?

"Must I?" I muttered, taking off my helmet and wishing I could have corrected him to call me Dirk. But then I remembered I called myself Wally to the police. It was getting hard to keep track of who I was.

"This is my Uncle Vinnie," Shard said. "He can fix anything."

Fiona looked unsure about letting him near her precious Ducati, but with his puppy-dog smile, I guess she found it hard to say no. She took the cover off the engine and pointed to something inside. They bent over it and I heard her say something about switches and wires and plugs. I had no idea what they were talking about. Vinnie loped back to the truck, opened the driver's side door and brought out a red toolbox.

"He's a mechanic?" I asked.

"No," Shard said, pointing to the side of the truck. "He's a baker."

On the side panel there was a huge picture of Vinnie, smiling of course, holding a basket of pastries with a banner over it that read *The Muffin Man*. Underneath the image were the words, *Now you know him.*

I'm not sure I wanted to know him.

"A baker who fixes motorcycles?"

"He's very handy," she said, folding her arms and daring me to argue with her.

I didn't. Besides, having a Mr. Fix-It uncle with his own business sure beat my uncle. My dad's brother was the world's worst minister. I say world's worst because he had been "let go" from five different congregations so far. How can you fail at being a minister? Well, if you're a Dearing, you can. Now he was the minister for prison inmates. I guess that was the only place where he wouldn't be fired.

Vinnie tinkered with Fiona's engine for a while longer, with her hovering over it like a mama bear and her cub.

Shard and I walked over. "Can you fix it?" I asked Vinnie.

"Oh, I can fix it all right," he told me. "If I had the part I needed. But this's gotta be ordered special. This here's no ordinary bike."

At that, Fiona beamed. It was odd to see her smile. It changed her face completely.

"So, what's the plan?" I asked. There was no way I was staying on the side of this deserted road any longer.

"Well, there's a little town a few kilometres down the road. We passed through it when we were looking for you. There's gotta be a garage there where they can help us," Vinnie said.

A few *kilometres* down the road? How were we going to push the bike for "a few kilometres"?

"Let's just get this baby loaded up and we'll be on our way," he said.

"Loaded up? Where? In the truck?" I asked.

Vinnie grinned and loped to the back of the bakery truck. He swung the doors open and the most heavenly smell of cinnamon and peaches and chocolate wafted out.

"Have you got room for her in there?" Fiona asked nervously.

"Oh, sure. I had just finished two stops when Shard called me," Vinnie said.

"Two stops?"

"Yup." Vinnie proudly pulled me around to the other side of the truck where I could see a window with a small ledge under it. "I drive around town and when I find a good spot, I pull over and open up my shop."

I went around to the back and peered inside. There was a long counter on the wall opposite the window, with cupboards above it. Under the counter was an oven, a small fridge and more storage. At the far end was an opening to the cab and on either side were big sacks of flour piled on the floor. On the wall with the window were rolling racks tied to the wall with bungee cords. And on every available countertop were plastic muffin trays stacked up. Some had slid onto the floor and Vinnie climbed in to tidy up.

He restacked the trays and shoved them into the cupboards.

"Okay, you two—" He pointed to Shard and me. "— hop in, and when we hoist the bike in there, you secure it to those rings on the walls with the extra bungee cords in that box over there, okay?"

Fiona paled a little, and I was about to argue that maybe we shouldn't be touching the Ducati, when Shard jumped in. I really had no choice, so I hopped up and joined her.

"Now, we're going to slide this beaut down the middle and you guys guide it in straight."

It was a delicate operation with Fiona having fits that the racks, the cupboards, the trays or the cords were going to scratch her precious Ducati. Finally it was all snug and tied down. We backed up into the cab but I saw that we had a problem. There were only two seats and four people.

"Uncle Vinnie?" Shard called. "Where should we sit? On the Ducati?"

"NO!" yelled Fiona. "There's no sitting on the Ducati."

"It's a motorbike. You're *supposed* to sit on it," I said.

"*I'm* supposed to sit on it," Fiona said. "No one is going to just 'hang out' on her."

"You can sit on the flour sacks," Vinnie said, a smile in his voice. "They're pretty comfortable."

"Isn't that illegal?" I asked, eyeing them. They looked about as comfortable as concrete blocks. And I wasn't too keen on staying in the back, closed in like that, either. Up front there were windows all around, and I wouldn't feel like the walls were closing in on me. The space in the back wasn't nearly as small as a trunk, but my heart was already starting to pound at the thought of those doors shutting.

"Nah. You're fine. Have a leftover muffin or two from the trays." With that he slammed the doors shut. He climbed in the cab with Fiona and turned the motor over. With a jerk, we started to move.

I tried to concentrate on keeping my balance on those rock-hard flour sacks with nothing to keep me from bouncing around the inside of the truck like a Ping-Pong ball.

"Are you okay?" Shard asked, probably hearing me breathing heavily.

"Sure," I said, pretending nothing was wrong. "Hey, I heard the word *muffin*, and I haven't eaten since Fiona and I had breakfast at the truck stop."

The big space and the window on the side for selling helped me keep my fears under control.

As soon as we were moving smoothly, I scooted over to the bungeed trays that were still lined with muffins.

"A Little Miss Muffin?" I said, reading the tag on the front of the tray. "What's in that?"

"I dunno," Shard said. "Curds and whey?" She rooted around in another tray. "I'm trying one of these Hot Cross Bunnies carrot muffins."

In the end, we tried one of every kind. My favourite was the Better Than Apple Pie muffin. It had a streusel topping with cinnamon and brown sugar. It really was better than an apple pie, in my opinion.

There was this question that had been on my mind most of the afternoon, but I hadn't asked Shard yet. Part of me didn't want to know and the other part was curious. Curiosity won out. "So, did Family Services come around again?" I asked.

Shard swallowed the last bite of a Grizzly Bear's Lunch muffin (blueberry and walnut). "Yeah. This morning. She seemed mad too. Told my parents she was going to charge them with obstruction or some garbage like that."

"Were your parents upset?" I asked. The last thing I wanted was for the Kents to get in trouble because of me.

"Nah. Mrs. Family Services was totally

out-manoeuvred by my folks. They've dealt with these government types for years. In the end, she was sweating pretty good as they questioned her about following the rules of apprehension of a minor or something. It was almost funny."

Shard chuckled, but I didn't feel like laughing. This Mrs. Family Services didn't sound like she was going to give up easily.

CHAPTER 16

THE ANSWER'S RIGHT IN FRONT OF YOU

We were bouncing around the back of the truck pretty good. Just how far was this town, anyway? Because it felt like we'd been doing this for hours. I would've asked, but Vinnie had the radio up pretty loud and was singing along at top volume. He wouldn't have heard explosives going off in the truck behind him.

Shard was talking up a storm, giving me the rundown on everyone in Sunnyview Terrace and what they were doing. I bet none of them were running from the law and planning to defraud the government by impersonating an adult.

I would have given anything to talk to my dad right then, but I knew from experience that you can't call anyone in jail. They have to call you, and to do that, you have to give them your phone number, which, of course, I couldn't do because

I didn't have a phone. And I wouldn't give him that number even if I did have one because all those crime shows I watched had taught me that they could find you using the GPS in your phone. I really didn't need to make this easier for Family Services. But I sure wanted to hear his voice and ask him how he was and whether or not I was doing the right thing.

Well, it was too late for that now.

"Looks like we're here," Shard said as the engine shut off.

I couldn't wait to get out of there. As soon as the doors opened, I took a deep breath.

"How is she?" Fiona asked, putting a hand on the back wheel of the Ducati.

"Fine. She had a few muffins and we played cards to pass the time," I said, too exhausted to hide my sarcasm.

"Ahahaha," Vinnie laughed, "that's a good one."

Fiona gave him a dirty look. "Just undo the bungees and be careful they don't snap back and scratch her." She wasn't happy until the Ducati was safe on the ground and she gave it a thorough inspection.

"Where are we?" I asked. I expected us to be parked in front of a gas station. Preferably one with a bathroom. This was a low white building, with several decrepit cars parked around the side, squatting between an old red-brick factory of some kind on one side and a grey stucco welding shop on the other.

"We couldn't find a garage in Hainsville, so we continued on to Strathcona," Vinnie said.

I'd never heard of Strathcona and could only hope it had a great garage that could fix the Ducati quickly. Shard and I sat on the back end of the open truck and waited while Vinnie and Fiona rolled the Ducati into the garage.

When they returned, the look on Fiona's face said it all. "They have to order the part," she said. "It could take up to two weeks because it has to come from Italy."

"Two weeks?" I yelled. "I can't wait that long. By then the claim will be gone."

"What claim?" Vinnie asked.

"His grandfather's gold claim in the Yukon," Shard said.

"Is that where you're going?" Vinnie asked me.

"Didn't Shard tell you?" I asked. I could only imagine what kind of story she used to get him to come.

"She just said her best friend was in trouble and needed my help. That was good enough for me," Vinnie said, his already wide smile growing even wider.

"Well, now what are we going to do?" I asked. Was everything going to be ruined because of one small motorcycle part?

"I vote we just turn around and go home," Fiona said.

"Isn't your mother expecting you?" I asked. I didn't humiliate myself shopping for pantyhose for nothing. "And Uncle Joey?"

"Oh, shoot. You're right." Fiona rolled her eyes.

"Why don't you just rent a car?" Shard asked.

Fiona looked horrified. "And what? Just leave the Ducati here? With strangers? No. Way."

We stood around looking miserable. What a mess. As if this whole thing wasn't hard enough without motorcycle troubles.

"It's easy," Vinnie said. "The answer's right in front of you!" He spread his arms wide and danced a little happy dance — right there in the parking lot.

We all stared at him. Had he completely lost his mind? Cars were honking their horns as they drove by. I wanted to climb back in the truck and hide.

"What are you talking about?" Fiona asked, one hand still on the Ducati.

"My truck, of course. It can take all of us AND the Ducati up north. Call ahead and get them to order the part and they can fix your bike when you get there. Easy peasy, lemon squeezy."

"Don't you have a business to run?" Fiona asked him.

"I'm mobile! The mobile muffin man! I can bake in my truck anytime and sell out my window anywhere I stop. And I feel a road trip coming on!" He jumped in the air, one arm pumped up as if he had just scored a game-winning basket.

More honks from cars driving by.

"What about Shard?" Fiona asked. "Won't her parents expect her back?"

"Shard's on a rescue mission with her favourite uncle," he said. "She's fighting a grave social injustice, battling government interference, sticking it to the man! And if I know my hippie-loving sister, she'd be riding with us, if she could."

We all looked at Shard. She shrugged. "Simple phone call will tell us," she said. "Besides, why should Chris get to have an adventure without me?" She punched me in the arm to make her point. I resisted the urge to rub it.

Was that what I was having? An adventure? Felt more like an act of desperation to me.

"Do you mean we have to load that thing back in the truck?" I asked. "And sit on flour sacks again?"

Vinnie rubbed his chin. "Hmm. You're right. It can't be good for the flour to have all that body heat on it. Might ruin the flour."

Ruin the flour? What about *my behind?* It felt like someone had been smacking it with a hard wooden paddle for three hours.

"Oh, I've got it!" Vinnie said with his ever-present grin on his face. He jumped through the big doors at the back of the truck and started moving stuff around. He rolled the metal racks closer together on one side and rearranged the flour sacks to make two flat benches on each side of the opening to the cab. Then he pulled down a couple of blankets from the cupboards and folded them on top of the hard flour bags.

"Ta-dah!" Vinnie said, grinning widely.

I had to admit, they looked pretty comfortable. I climbed up and wiggled around.

"Thanks, Vinnie," I said. "Just don't slam into anything because we don't have seat belts."

"Well, if the cops stop us, you two hide in the cupboards." Vinnie said this with a laugh like he was joking. I wasn't laughing. If it came down to it, I would have to choose between climbing into a suffocating cupboard where I would absolutely have another panic attack, or being picked up by the police and thrown into foster care where any chance of a future with my dad would disappear faster than a cockroach down a drain. I don't know what I would choose and just prayed it would never come to that.

Shard borrowed Fiona's phone to call her parents. Vinnie was right. They were happy I was "escaping the clutches of bureaucratic incompetence," whatever that means, and even said they would run interference for me if Family Services came knocking again. We helped tie down the Ducati and hit the road. We only stopped once for some fast-food burgers and fries, and then kept on going. Vinnie and Fiona decided to take turns and drive all night, seeing as we lost so much time with the breakdown and the garage. That was fine with me now that I had my flour-sack bed.

Besides, all the bad luck was behind us. Right?

CHAPTER 17

THE SECRET WEAPON

I didn't feel all the bumps and swerves of our night drive, but my body did. I had so many sore muscles and bruises from those rotten flour sacks that I felt like an apple that had been dropped on the floor and kicked around the cafeteria for a while.

Shard was still sleeping on her sacks. I sat up and poked my head through the doorway to the cab. The sky was just turning a violet colour out the passenger-side window. Fiona was driving. Vinnic was snoozing.

"Where are we?" I whispered.

"The middle of nowhere," Fiona said in a low voice.

"That narrows it down," I said, lying back down on my concrete bed. I hoped we were going to stop soon. I desperately wanted to walk around on ground that didn't jiggle.

It took a while, but the truck finally began to slow and turn. The sun was up, and so were Vinnie and Shard. Everyone was groggy. And grumpy. Was I really the only morning person here?

We were at one of those highway gas stations, because Fiona said we had been running on fumes for the last twenty minutes. Shard and I climbed out through the cab to stretch our legs and use the bathroom.

When we got back to the truck Vinnie was there with two coffees and two juices.

"Guava?" I said, reading the label. "You got me guava juice?"

"It's guava and strawberry. Very good for you," Vinnie said.

If it was so good for you, why wasn't he drinking it? I took a swig and shuddered. It was gross — something like a cross between an underripe strawberry and a watered-down pineapple.

Worse than that, the drink woke my stomach up and it growled pretty loud. Fiona raised her eyebrows. "Hungry?"

I shrugged. I was still trying to save my money for the claim fees.

"I'm starving," Shard said.

"Sorry, guys. This truck guzzles gas and this is the third time I've filled it since last night," Fiona said. "We can make do with leftover muffins for breakfast. We need cash to put gas in the tank and I've got to save some money for the repair bill."

Vinnie opened his wallet and then closed it again quickly. Shard shrugged. We were a great bunch. No one had enough gas money to get us north.

Vinnie smiled and spread his arms. "Breakfast is on me!" No one said anything. "Come on, everyone in the truck."

We all climbed back into our spots, this time with Vinnie at the wheel and Fiona collapsing in the passenger seat. We didn't go back on the highway, but instead drove into whatever city this was. It was bigger than Strathcona and the downtown had office buildings on both sides of the street, blocking out the sun. I don't know how the scrawny trees that were planted in gaps in the sidewalk managed to survive.

It seemed like every time I climbed out of the truck the landscape had changed entirely — from dark, swampy forests to sleepy small towns to rows of wheat swaying in the wind to the metal and glass of towering office buildings.

Vinnie seemed to be going pretty slow and making a lot of turns, as if he were looking for something. I craned my neck to see out the little service window.

He finally screeched to a stop by a small grassy square that I guess was supposed to be a park. Nobody was using it though; everyone I could see was walking, heads down and hanging on to purses and briefcases.

"Here we are!" Vinnie said, getting out.

I didn't know what Vinnie was up to, but we were parked on a street with no restaurants. Where was breakfast?

"Help me get the bike out, Chris," Vinnie said.

At the word "bike" Fiona sat bolt upright. "What are you doing?" she asked in a panicked voice.

"Just moving the bike out of my kitchen," Vinnie said.

Shard undid all the ties while Vinnie and I opened the back doors and pulled the Ducati out onto the road. Fiona took it from us the minute the front wheel touched the pavement, rolled it over to a bench in the park and sat down.

Vinnie climbed in the back, opened the cupboards and took out bowls, pans, wooden spoons and an apron. He grabbed one of the sacks of flour from Shard's bed and pulled out plastic containers with other white powders in them. He opened the tiny fridge and I saw eggs, milk and fruit. It didn't take a genius to realize he was going to bake muffins.

"We still have a couple of muffins left over from yesterday," I said.

"That's not enough to earn us gas money," Vinnie said. "We'll sell those as 'day-olds' but we need fresh ones if this quest is going to be successful."

Quest? First it's an adventure and now it's a quest? This might be all fun and games to them, but this was my life. My future. Not some game.

I couldn't be mad though. Vinnie and Shard had come through when I really needed them. So, if we needed to make muffins to make this work, then pass me a wooden spoon. I jumped in and asked what I could do.

"There are plastic containers in that cupboard," Vinnie said. "You can package up the 'day-olds' for now. Shard, maybe you could pull out that whiteboard there and start making the menu sign for today."

Out the back doors I could see Fiona sitting on the bench, fiddling with her phone.

"I'll be right back," I told Vinnie, and jumped out.

"Can you do me a favour?" I asked her when I got near.

Fiona made a face. "Haven't you had enough favours lately?"

"Yeah. But could I ask for one more?"

Fiona sighed. "What is it?"

"Can you call my dad?"

"You can't call someone in jail," she said.

"I know. But we could find out if he's still locked up or out already. If he was released, he could be on his way up to meet us."

"Here, call yourself." She held her phone out to me.

"I can't," I said. "They'll ask where I am, or check the GPS or something if they know it's me."

Fiona shook her head and then asked me where he was. It was probably the thought that if my dad was out and could come, then she could go home again and be rid of me that made her look up the number on her screen and then dial it.

"Marlin Correctional Facility," I could hear a voice say, even though Fiona was holding the phone to her ear. I leaned in closer.

"Yes, hello. I'm trying to find out if you have a prisoner there named Frank Dearing . . ." Fiona said, trying to shoo me away.

"Francis!" I whispered frantically. "His real name is Francis."

". . . er, Francis Dearing."

"We don't give out information over the phone," the voice said.

"Oh, right," Fiona said. "It's just that I've been

asked to take over his case because his original lawyer got sick, and his handwriting is impossible to read in his notes so I wasn't sure which correctional facility he was being held in." Did I mention what a great liar she was?

"Oh, well, I still shouldn't, but seeing as you're his legal counsel . . ." There was silence. "Yes, he's here."

"Oh, great. I'll head over then."

"Wait a minute," the voice said. "I have a note here on his file that his son is missing. Do you know where he is?"

I felt all the blood drain from my face.

"No, but I'll ask around," Fiona said and hung up.

She didn't say anything to me, and I didn't feel like saying anything to her. I just went back to the truck. I was still on my own.

When I climbed back in, Vinnie was pouring batter into muffin cups. "Bears in a Bathtub, Polka-Dot muffins, Cosmic muffins and, um, maybe some Lemon Liftoff muffins," he said.

Shard rolled her eyes but wrote them all down on the whiteboard.

"What are Bear in a Bathtub muffins?" I had to ask.

"You'll see," Vinnie said, moving at warp speed from the counter to the oven to the racks.

"And now, for my secret weapon."

Vinnie reached up over the oven to the vent that went to the outside and slid a lever to the left. "Aaaaaah," he said. "The heavenly smell of my muffins will call to the people and they will come to the Muffin Man." He laughed.

You know what's weird? His secret weapon worked. That smell of baking chocolate and cinnamon and lemon was like the Pied Piper of aromas. I watched out the back of the truck. You could see people's heads come up, their eyebrows crinkle and their eyes dart around looking for the source. Then you could see them read the side of the truck, smile and come over.

Shard ran the cash while I packaged up the warm muffins. Vinnie was still moving like a blur. Fiona was still on the bench outside, ignoring us.

That lineup never stopped for what seemed like hours. Vinnie just kept mixing, stirring and baking. Shard and I snacked on the muffin mistakes — the ones that broke when they came out of the pan. When there was finally a break in the customers, I looked at the clock over Vinnie's window. It was eleven thirty.

Vinnie stuck his head out the window and looked up and down the street. "I'll just wait for the last few customers as I clean up," he said to us, pulling his head back in. "Why don't you two take a break?"

He didn't have to tell me twice. I was exhausted. Fiona was still on the bench, both legs draped over the seat of the Ducati, her head back, mouth open, asleep. I didn't kid myself though. If someone so much as stared too long at that bike, she'd feel it and wake up.

Shard and I walked down the street, looking in the lobbies of the office buildings and in the fronts of the photocopy shops, dry cleaners and florists.

"Where did Vinnie learn to bake?" I asked.

"Oh, in an old-folks' home."

"He was the cook in a seniors' place?" Somehow I couldn't picture Vinnie making daily vats of Jell-O and rice pudding. He was too, I don't know, *creative* for that.

"Not really," Shard said, looking a bit uncomfortable. "He did some community service there."

"Community service? As in, punishment for getting arrested?"

Shard nodded.

I laughed. NOW we were talking my kind of relatives. "What did he do?"

"It was a disorderly conduct charge."

"Okay. But what did he do?" I tried to picture what sort of crime Vinnie would commit: Peeing on a street corner? Swearing at a bus driver? Inciting a riot? What?

"He, uh, was holding up traffic in a big intersection."

"Holding it up? Doing what?"

Shard winced. "Singing Italian opera for money."

I laughed again. I didn't see that coming. "So he gets community service in an old-age home and learns to bake?"

It was a great story. Shard and I joked about our relatives all the way back to the muffin truck. As we got close, a silver car slowed as it passed by, and I glanced over. My eyes locked with the driver's.

It felt like icy cold fingers were clawing down my back.

The driver was Randy the wallet thief.

CHAPTER 18

COPS HAVE LONG MEMORIES

"What is *he* doing here?" I said, my voice quivering a bit as I watched the car slowly continue down the street and then turn the corner.

"Who?" Shard asked, looking around.

"The driver of the silver car that just went by . . . it was the guy who came to our apartment that night and started asking all those questions about my grandfather's claim."

"No. It couldn't be. I'm sure it was just someone who reminded you of him. What would he be doing here in . . . where are we again?"

I couldn't tell her — some big, nondescript city with doppelganger wallet thieves driving around. I wanted so badly to believe Shard that it was just a guy who looked like Randy, but if I listened to deep down in my gut, which was churning like a cement mixer, I'd know I was right. I could only hope he didn't see Fiona sitting in the little park and realize that I was riding with the Muffin Man. That truck wasn't exactly camouflaged.

Vinnie was just wiping down the stove and counters when we climbed back in.

"So, how'd we do?" Shard asked.

Vinnie held up a grey metal cash box and shook it like maracas so the coins rattled. Then he jumped up and clicked his heels. You know, you had to smile when you were around Vinnie. He was just so darn happy.

"A bunch of coins aren't going to buy us supper and gas," Shard grumbled.

"The bills are already put away in my secret lockbox," Vinnie said. "Let's load up the bike and hit the road!"

I couldn't help glancing up and down the street before I jumped out to get Fiona, just to make sure the silver car wasn't lurking just up the street. It wasn't.

Fiona was awake again and back on her phone.

"News from home?" I asked, hoping it wasn't her mother telling her not to bother coming, that Uncle Joey was already floating down the river.

"It's Lisa."

"Oh. How are things at the Bull?"

"Well, last night there were two fights, one

arrest, a broken lamp and six smashed glasses . . . all in all, a pretty quiet night."

Really? What was a rowdy night like?

"We're ready to hit the road," I said.

Fiona put her phone in her pocket. "Coming."

Vinnie was in a great mood when we pulled out. My mood wasn't bad either, seeing as we were finally moving again. There was just that little worry about the "Randy Incident," but maybe Shard was right: maybe it was just his look-alike.

I can't believe I'm saying this, but I was getting used to the bumpy ride on blankets over flour sacks. Shard and I even managed to have a card game, using one of the flat metal baking trays as a table.

We made only one quick stop at a mini-mart, and while Vinnie loaded up on baking supplies we grabbed some subs for lunch. Then it was back on the road. We were off the main highway now and mostly going through small towns on two-lane country roads. It was slower going but every hour brought me closer to my new future, and with all the delays so far, we needed to make tracks.

"Have you figured out how you're going to register the claim yet?" Shard asked. "What if they ask for ID?"

"Maybe I'll get a fake ID with my dad's name on it."

With anyone else, the reaction I'd get would be something about it being illegal, or getting in trouble, or what if I get caught. All Shard said was, "You'll need to forge his signature. Are you any good?" This is why Shard and I are best friends. She understands that in our world you do whatever you have to to survive.

"I'm not sure. I know what it's supposed to look like, though." I pulled out the registration form that had my dad's signature on it, to copy.

"So let's see how well you do," she said.

It wasn't easy in the back of a muffin truck, using only a baking sheet for a table and an old receipt and pencil that we found in a drawer. But even with the bouncing motion, I thought I did a pretty good job.

"I think the loop looks too, I don't know, loopy," Shard said.

I tried again, making my "g" loop a little flatter.

"Hmmm, now your 'D' looks too curvy," Shard said, holding the receipt up.

"What are you guys doing?" Fiona asked, leaning over to look into the back of the truck.

I wasn't going to say what we were doing because I was kind of embarrassed that I wasn't more prepared for all this, but Shard told her.

Fiona reached back and asked for the receipt and the document. "No, this is all wrong," she said, and bent over the paper. When she handed the receipt back there was a perfect copy of the way my dad signed his name.

"How did you do that?" I asked her.

Fiona looked for a second like she wasn't going to answer but then just said, "Talent of mine."

Shard and I studied the signature. "You've got some practising to do," she said to me.

"Yeah, but I'm sure I can get it close enough."

"Now you only have one small problem."

"And that is?"

"You don't look like a forty-year-old man. Or did you think you could just stand in front of the registrar and pass over ID that says you're your dad?"

Have I ever mentioned how much I hate it when Shard is right?

"I haven't worked that out yet," I said. "Maybe I can pretend he's outside in a car, sick, and can't come in?"

"Unless there's a window in the office that the guy can look out of."

I crumpled the paper and threw it at her. I would have to think of a solution later, because right then I heard Vinnie say something I hoped he never would.

"Cops." And then he swore. With a family full of losers, drunks and convicts, I'd heard my share of swearing over the years. While I think Fiona had a better swear vocabulary, Vinnie swore loudly, with a lot of emotion. It was quite impressive.

"What do you mean, cops?" I asked, already knowing the answer.

"A cruiser passed by us, and now he's pulled a U-ey and is following us."

This was it. I'd be hauled off to foster care before I could get up north and fix things for my dad and me. "I knew they wouldn't stop looking for me," I said, hitting the side of the truck in anger.

"You?" Vinnie said. "They ain't looking for you, kid. They're looking for me."

"What did YOU do?" Shard asked. "Mom said you had learned your lesson and were going to fly straight."

"I did. I did. It's just that a roadside vending licence costs money, and I was kinda waiting until I got my business rolling."

"Oh, great!" I said. "Now they're going to catch me because you didn't register as the Muffin Man. Perfect."

"How would they know whether or not you have your licence, anyway? We're hours past that city we were in this morning," Shard said.

"They wouldn't," Fiona answered her. We

poked our heads through the doorway and saw Fiona shaking her head. "And they don't know you're in here, either, Chris."

"So who are they after?" Shard asked.

"Me," Fiona said.

"You?!" the three of us said at the same time.

"What did YOU do?" I asked.

"Well, we're getting pretty close to Edmonton and I kinda had a run-in with the law here a few years back."

"What kind of 'run-in'?" Vinnie asked, looking back and forth between his side-view mirror and the road.

"Gang stuff."

"You mean when you were in a motorcycle gang?" I asked. Fiona nodded. "But you got out! You run a respectable, well, profitable business now!"

"Doesn't matter. Cops got long memories, and that one had a good look at me as he went by us the first time. Looks like my past has caught up to me and they're going to bring me in."

"Not if I have something to say about it," Vinnie said. He pressed on the accelerator.

"Are you sure you know what you're doing?" Fiona asked.

"This ain't my first rodeo," Vinnie answered. "Hang on!"

Really? Hang on to what? The truck made a sharp right turn and I was thrown on top of Shard.

"Sorry! Sorry!" I said.

"Watch the hands, mister!"

Then the truck veered to the left, and we were both thrown to the other side. I bumped my head on the front wheel of the bike. I hoped Fiona didn't see that.

"They're still following us," I heard Fiona say.

"Not for long." Vinnie put the pedal to the floor and the poor old truck's engine screeched in protest. I was gripping one of the racks that was tied to the wall. Shard was gripping my leg.

We swerved left, then right, then a harder right. I'm sure running from the cops was a bad idea. But no worse than getting put into the system because Fiona made some mistakes in her past. Or because Vinnie was a lazy entrepreneur.

I could hear the crunch of gravel under the tires; we were obviously on a dirt road now. But I never did hear any sirens. That was good, right?

Now tree branches were hitting the sides of the truck too. Where were we? All of a sudden, the truck screeched to a halt. None of us moved.

We all strained to listen. There was a car engine that went by, but it was a ways away by the sound of it. When it died down, I got up from the floor, pried Shard's hands off my leg and crawled into the cab.

"Are we safe?"

"Safe as in your mother's arms," Vinnie said.

How safe was that, exactly? What if those arms were wrapped around you like a warm blanket one day but were pulling the covers up over her head while she spent the day in bed the next? I wished he had said we were as safe as a tortoise under its shell or something. Then maybe I could stop shaking.

I got up from my crouching position and saw that we had pulled into a campground. It was mostly empty, but there were a couple of tents set up farther down the road. Where Vinnie had parked, the trees and bushes completely hid us from the road that ran past the camp.

"I think maybe we'll spend the night here," he said. No one argued. I was bruised and sweating from the ride.

"Don't you think they'll check here eventually?" Shard asked.

"Nah, we lost the copper back on the county road. We're good for the night. I'll just go and make arrangements with the camp office."

Vinnie hopped out and headed off. He was back in a few minutes and put a white paper in the windshield.

"I need to find a bathroom," Fiona said.

"I need food," Shard said.

"Food is coming up. Just need to get this motorbike out of my kitchen," Vinnie said.

"Uh, Uncle Vinnie? No offence, but I don't think I could eat muffins again today."

"What's wrong with muffins?" Vinnie asked, untying the Ducati. "But no, we won't have more muffins."

We got the bike out and Vinnie climbed in and opened one of the top cupboards. He pulled out a couple of cans triumphantly. "Beaners and wieners!" he said.

I was about to say how good that sounded. I mean, really, when a lot of your suppers are pickles and saltine crackers, baked beans and hot dogs sounds like a feast. But Shard reached up and started opening up the rest of the cupboards.

"Why've you got cans of beans in here? And toothpaste. And clothes?" Shard turned to Vinnie with a look of horror on her face. "Are you living in here?!"

Vinnie shrugged. "It's just for a while."

"What happened to your apartment?"

"Had a little trouble paying the rent on time," he said. I felt for the guy. That was my dad's problem too. "Don't worry, I'll get another one as soon as my business is on its feet. Why don't you guys stretch your legs a bit while I warm this feast up?"

Shard and I staggered outside and collapsed on the picnic table that came with the campsite. Fiona wandered back and climbed into the truck to help with supper, I guess.

"I still don't get it," Shard said.

"Get what?" I asked, rubbing my bruised knees.

"Why Fiona agreed to take you up here. I mean, she's got a business to run, she doesn't get along with her family, she's got trouble with the police, not to mention an old motorbike gang, but she dropped everything to bring you up here after looking at some dumb old photo of your granddad? It just doesn't make any sense."

"It wasn't the photo. Don't forget about Uncle Joey. You are asking for paranormal trouble from a restless spirit if you don't fufill their dying wishes."

"She can do that any time. Ashes aren't going anywhere."

"So she's got a conscience. Is that such a bad thing?" I was getting edgy. I was trying to trust Fiona. Trust that she wasn't taking me up north to get her hands on Granddad's claim herself. I mean, she said she knew all about him and the claim. Now she knows the claim is about to be up for grabs. What's to stop her from ditching me somewhere and taking it for herself? I was talking myself into a nervous breakdown. I had to trust Fiona. I had no choice.

Shard didn't have to, though. She made a sound like a tire deflating. "Face it, forger boy, there's something else going on here."

I really, really hoped this was one of the rare times when Shard was wrong.

CHAPTER 19

WILL YOU BE MY DAD?

Who would have thought that the floor would be more comfortable than flour sacks? Me. Which is why I slept on a blanket in the doorway to the cab. When I woke up, Fiona was curled up on the passenger seat, Shard was on her flour-sack sofa and Vinnie was missing.

I crawled up the driver's seat and tried to look out the window. I guess as we went farther north, even at the end of June, the nights could still be chilly and our body heat had caused the windows to fog up. I wiped a circle with my hand and saw that Vinnie was sitting at the picnic table reading a paper. My scrambling around woke Fiona.

"This trip is like every camping nightmare I've ever had, come to life. All I need now is for a giant spider to crawl out of the dashboard vents," she said.

I couldn't help it. I had to look at the dashboard vents, you know, just in case. Fiona scowled. I opened the driver's side door as quietly as I could, so as not to wake Shard, and got out.

"Top o' the morning!" Vinnie said in an Irish accent.

"Morning. Uh, where's the bathroom?" I asked. Last night it was so dark with no street lights that I didn't have the nerve to walk by myself across the mostly empty campground and had to resort to the bushes at the back of our site.

"Vault toilet is at the end of this road, on your right."

Vault toilet? What was a vault toilet? Please tell me it was just a nice bathroom with a really, really tall ceiling.

It wasn't. A vault toilet is a fancy name for a latrine . . . you know, a wooden hut built over a large hole in the ground. I was so grossed out. I made a promise never to complain about real bathrooms again, no matter how old, cramped and smelly they were.

When I got back, there was an unmistakable smell of eggs and bacon. Shard was sitting at the picnic table, head down in her folded arms.

"Morning," I said.

"*Mmmp,*" came the reply. She was so not a morning person.

I walked around to the back of the truck and almost collided with Vinnie as he came out holding two plates of muffins. I poked my head around the corner, looking for the eggs and bacon. Nothing was on the stove. Back at the picnic table, Fiona passed out some napkins. The smell was definitely coming from the table, but all I could see were muffins.

"Come on, Chris, dig in. These are my Breakfast Bonanza muffins. I just made them up: hash brown bottom and scrambled eggs with bacon on top. I melted cheese on a few too," Vinnie said.

There's no way I would have thought of cooking breakfast in a muffin tin, but it was actually delicious. "You should put these on the menu. People would go crazy for them."

"You think so?" Vinnie asked, smiling. "Well, you just never know where you're gonna find inspiration."

"Yeah, who would have thought running from the police while taking a fugitive north would be so good for business," Fiona said sarcastically.

"So, what's the plan?" Shard asked, reaching for a second Breakfast Bonanza.

"Well, I was thinking that since most of us in our little group would rather not run into the police again . . ." Vinnie paused and looked at the rest of us. We all nodded. No one wanted another scary drive like yesterday. ". . . we'll stick to some quieter back roads from now on. It'll take a bit longer, so why don't we clean up and get going. Maybe use the bathroom once more before we hit the road so we don't have to stop for a while."

It only took a few minutes to put everything away and tie up the Ducati again. I passed on the bathroom break, but Shard went. When she came back she looked like she was gagging. I decided to just try and hold it until the next gas station.

As we pulled out, I heard *pings* on the metal truck roof that got faster and harder as we got moving. I was happy to hear the rain. I hoped the downpour would hide us a bit by keeping people off the streets. Maybe the cops would decide to stay inside in a doughnut shop drinking a hot coffee too, instead of patrolling the highways, looking for criminal bakers, bikers and runaway minors.

Of course, hard rain hides other things — like highway numbers and signposts. After a few hours of backcountry roads and hundreds of turns, it became obvious from the yelling and swearing, which I could hear over the rain pounding on the metal roof overhead, that we were lost.

"No! Left on Highway 49 — left!" Fiona said, raising her voice to a scream.

"That wasn't Highway 49," Vinnie said, matching her in volume. "That was 35 and we're still going north."

"No, we're heading east! Turn around."

"I can't turn this thing around on such a narrow road. And I can barely see the shoulders in this rain."

Fiona's answer was some kind of *arrrrgh*.

Somehow we seemed to get back on track, heading north. Lunch was hot dogs from a roadside truck. It should have taken us only a few minutes to get our foil-wrapped dogs, but Vinnie got into a conversation with the owner about the ups and downs of a food-truck business. Vinnie got me to reach around the bike to get some of the day-old muffins, which he traded for spicy beef and olives. I couldn't imagine what kind of muffins he was planning on making with those.

I wished he'd hurry up. I hated being impatient, but this trip had already dragged on for so long. I just wanted to get up there and get it all over with. Besides, I was starting to come up with a plan about how to get around the age thing — I was going to ask, well, beg Vinnie to pretend to be my dad.

It's a pretty good plan, don't you think? I was

sure I could trust him. Vinnie was too nice a guy to steal the claim from us. And as for looks, they're roughly the same age and height, not that that really matters. It's not like we'd ever have to see the registrar again.

I had one little problem with this plan: I had to convince Vinnie to impersonate my dad in a government office, which was, well, illegal. Okay, so it was a big problem. But at least I wouldn't have to try and find somewhere to buy a fake ID and forge my dad's signature. And really, for a guy who was driving around selling muffins without a licence and living out of a food truck, I didn't think he'd be too fussy about handing over a form pretending to be someone else.

It was really, really late when we pulled into another secluded campground for the night. Fiona said we were about ten or eleven hours out of Dawson, and she and Vinnie were too tired to drive all night. Vinnie sprung for some firewood at the camp office, and supper was reheated spicy beef from the hot dog stand and more baked beans.

"Is this all you have? Cans of baked beans?" Shard asked her uncle.

Vinnie looked down at his bowl and then said in a small voice, "They were on sale. Besides, I like baked beans."

"Yes, but *every day*?"

"You know," Fiona jumped in, "when my business was just starting up and I was fixing motorcycles in the back alley between drink orders just to scrape enough money together for the rent, I lived on nothing but ramen noodles for five months. I would have killed for a can of beans."

Vinnie looked up at her in surprise and gave her a lopsided grin. Fiona held up her bowl to clink it with his in solidarity.

"Oh man," Shard whispered to me, "is this going to be one of those 'we walked ten miles to school in minus-thirty-degree temperatures, uphill both ways' speeches?"

I nodded, because Vinnie and Fiona had started trading stories about how tough they had it. He picked empty wine bottles out of recycling bins to get the deposit back and she washed her clothes in the kitchen sink with dish soap. He once had a beard for eight months because he couldn't afford razor blades and she used crazy glue and tire patch kits to fix holes in her shoes. I tuned it out after a while. Who needed to be reminded about what it was like to be poor? I was trying to get away from that, not relive it.

So we'd be in Dawson tomorrow. I only had one more day to talk to Vinnie about my plan.

I didn't know how to bring it up with him, but I knew there was someone who could help me with that.

"So, your Uncle Vinnie," I said to Shard. We were walking to the regular indoor bathrooms in the campground after supper, while Vinnie and Fiona tidied up. "He's a pretty helpful guy, right?"

"You want him to impersonate your dad for the claim, huh?"

How did she do that? Could she read minds or something? "Well, yeah. Do you think he would?"

Shard didn't answer right away. Instead she asked, "What will you do if he doesn't?"

Good question. Right now I didn't have a Plan B. I didn't know anyone else in Dawson — especially anyone I could trust.

"I'd have to figure out a way to do it myself," I said.

Shard made a face. "We both know how that would turn out."

Yeah. Not good. "So, will he?"

Shard shrugged. "How should I know? Ask him."

"I will, but what's the best way to go about it to, you know, win him over?"

"I don't know. Just ask him straight up. He

doesn't have the longest attention span."

Great. I hoped if he agreed to do it his attention would last long enough for him to remember to answer questions as "Francis Dearing."

I didn't want to do anything in front of Fiona, in case it all fell apart and then she wondered why she bothered to bring me up here. So I waited until she headed off to the bathrooms to brush her teeth and Vinnie was alone by the dying campfire.

"Hey, Vinnie, can I ask you something?"

"Sure."

"I kind of need a favour."

"Okay."

"You see, my dad was supposed to meet me up here."

"But he's still in prison."

"Yeah, how'd you know that?"

"Shard told me."

"Oh. Well, he's going to be out in a week or so. He was supposed to hand over some papers in Dawson. I'm too young to do it."

"The registration for the claim," Vinnie said, matter-of-factly.

"Right," I said, wondering how to word the next part.

"And you want me to pretend to be your dad."

Did psychic mind reading run in the family? "Uh, yeah." There was a long, awkward silence.

"So, do you think you could help me out?"

"Sure."

Was it really that easy? Was Vinnie so kind hearted, or was there some other reason he agreed so quickly? I shook my head. I had to stop being so suspicious. But I wondered, should I remind him it was illegal and that he could get in trouble for this? Nope. Because I didn't have a Plan B.

"Great. Thanks a lot. 'Night," I said, heading back to the truck.

"'Night."

Well, at least there was some hope now that I could pull this off. All I had to do was get to Dawson, have Vinnie register the claim and wait for my dad. Totally doable.

As long as nothing else happened.

CHAPTER 20
STICKY FINGERS

I was impatient to get going the next morning, but everyone else seemed to be moving in slow motion. And then Vinnie mentioned that he was out of money again and needed to stop and sell a few muffins when we got to Whitehorse. I would have banged my head against the truck wall in frustration if it would have done any good. I reminded myself that I owed Vinnie a lot for getting me up here, but to be so close and still not get on with the job of getting the claim drove me crazy.

We made good time to Whitehorse and I was eager to see what the capital city of the Yukon looked like. It wasn't a city like I was used to — it was too clean. A lot of the buildings were painted bright colours and there were banners on the street light poles. The sky had cleared and in the distance were mountains still covered with snow, making the whole thing look like a postcard.

Vinnie parked the truck across the street from a statue of a gold miner and his dog. I told myself it was a sign that everything was going to work out for me and my dad. Knowing that he didn't have a licence, I was a little nervous now about Vinnie selling on the street. If the cops came by, I would have to hide somewhere.

Vinnie got busy mixing and measuring, and before long the smells started coming out of the vent and wafting down the street. Shard pulled out the whiteboard sign again and wrote: *Golden Ticket muffins* (carrot-walnut muffins that were a beautiful orangey yellow), *Nugget muffins* (peanut butter muffins with big chunks of chocolate) and *Strike It Rich! muffins* (lemon, coconut and pecan muffins).

You know, Vinnie looked and acted a bit goofy, but he was a marketing genius. People smelled those muffins, and when they came to the window they loved the names of the muffins so much, most people walked away with a box of six — two of each.

I didn't have to package this time because Fiona was inside helping Vinnie. She had bungeed the Ducati to the open back doors of the truck. The two of them were laughing and nudging each other all morning. Gave me hives. I stayed outside on a bench, acting as lookout. Truth was, if a cop did come around, I planned on giving the alarm whistle we'd arranged and then taking off. I hadn't come this close to be caught now.

There was a steady stream of people, and at this rate, we'd be back on the road within the hour. I scanned the area looking for white cars with narrow red, yellow, white and blue stripes down the side — the local RCMP cruisers. It was a pretty good camouflage — all that white probably made the cars practically invisible in the winter.

"I can't stand it anymore." Shard had come out to the bench and flopped down.

"What?"

"Uncle Vinnie and Fiona: all the inside jokes, the smiley faces. There's just something weird about Fiona smiling all the time." Shard shuddered.

"Why have you got Fiona's phone?"

"I promised my mom that I would call every day or so."

I was about to tell her to say hi from me when something caught my eye: a silver car driving slowly down the street toward the Muffin Man truck. I pulled Shard off the bench and behind a shrub in a small garden bed.

"What are you doing?!" Shard asked, rubbing her arm. "You nearly pulled my arm out of the socket."

"It's that car again, the silver one I saw two days ago. And look, the driver *is* Randy. I wasn't imagining it. He's following us."

Shard stared at the car and driver from behind the shrub branches.

"I know him!" she said.

"You know Randy? From where?"

"Let me think. It was at the track."

"The racetrack?"

"Yeah, Dad used to take us there when he was supposed to be babysitting us — until Mom found out that he was gambling again. I haven't been in a while, but me and Merle and Reese would sit in the seats and share a pop while Dad did his betting thing. One time there was this big commotion. Security guards swooped in and arrested this guy for pickpocketing. It was better than a TV show. And the guy they arrested was him — Randy. I'm sure it's the same guy."

"A pickpocket? Well, that fits. I thought my dad must have left his wallet on the chair or table in the bar, but Randy probably lifted it right off him. And now he's up here, after my granddad's claim."

"One thing's for sure — that guy's bad news," Shard said.

"So what are we going to do? I can't just lead him right to the claim."

Shard was quiet for a minute, but I could almost hear her mind whirring as she thought. "One thing I've learned is, people rarely change," she said finally. "Randy obviously still has sticky fingers. Once a pickpocket, always a pickpocket."

"So?"

"Let's see where he goes."

"We're on foot — he's in a car. We'll never keep up," I said.

"Look, Whitehorse isn't that big and if he is checking you out, he's not going to go far."

I shrugged. It's not like I had a better idea. We followed the car, which luckily was still going fairly slowly, by staying behind other pedestrians. The silver car came to a stop at the lights at the end of the street, then turned left. We hurried ahead to try and keep an eye on it. Luck was with us, because just down the street, it turned into a doughnut shop.

We jogged to get closer and saw Randy go inside the shop. From behind a parked pickup truck we could see him clearly through the floor to ceiling windows, standing in line.

"He must have realized from the lineup outside

the muffin truck that we won't be leaving for a while and decided to grab a coffee," I said.

"That's not all he decided to grab," Shard said. "Look, he just lifted a wallet from that woman in front of him. I told you, once a pickpocket . . ."

"I didn't see anything."

"Well, I did." Shard pulled Fiona's phone from her pocket and started dialling.

"Who are you calling?"

"The cops, dingbat. This is our chance to stall him, at least long enough for us to head down the road without him following us."

She dialled 911. "Yes, I'd like to report a robbery . . . yup . . . at the doughnut shop on Main and—

"What street is that?" Shard whispered to me.

"Third Avenue."

"Main and Third." She gave the dispatcher a detailed description, then said goodbye.

"Are they coming?" I asked.

"Yup, and we're getting out of here." Shard put the phone back in her pocket and started walking quickly back the way we came. I had to jog to catch up with her. I could only hope Randy was still in there when the cops came and that Shard was right and that lady's wallet was in his pocket.

When we got to the corner, we stopped. There

was already a cruiser pulling into the parking lot. I guess that's the benefit of living in a smaller town — the cops are never far away. Mind you, that wasn't a benefit when you were running from the law.

"Shouldn't we go?" I asked, nervous that I'd be spotted by the police.

"Wait. Oh man, look! He's just strolling out. They're talking to the wrong guy." She punched me in the arm.

"Hey, what was that for?"

"I'm just frustrated. He's such a slippery eel."

Even from a distance you could see Randy scanning the area. Then Randy looked up, right in our direction.

"Let's get out of here," I said.

"Stop panicking. He doesn't know we saw him, and Vinnie will make sure we're not being followed."

Oh, how I wanted to believe her, but I knew that Randy must have researched where Cottonwood Creek was. And worse than that, I was pretty sure he had seen Shard and me on the street just now.

I felt sick to my stomach. We hadn't slowed Randy down at all. Would he beat me to the claim?

CHAPTER 21

VIKINGS IN THE YUKON

S hard was talking to me over the drone of the truck's engine but I wasn't listening. My heart was thudding in my chest. I had just seen the sign that read *Welcome to Dawson*. We were here.

"So, where's this Mining Recorder Office?" Vinnie called back to us.

"Forget that," Fiona said. "Take me to Lefty's garage to get my baby fixed. Who's more important here?"

They both laughed at that in the cab. Shard pointed her finger down her throat. I stifled a laugh.

"We googled it," I said. "It's on Front Street."

"Do you need me now?" Vinnie asked.

"No, I have to get the claim tags, find the claim and stake it, first," I said. It all sounded so normal when you just said it. Doing it was going to be something else again.

"So maybe just drop me off there," I said. "And then we'll drive out to the claim."

"Garage," said Fiona again.

"We'll drop you off at the garage," Vinnie said, giving Fiona a big smile, "Chris at the registry place and what about you, Shard?"

"I'll go with Chris. Make sure he doesn't forget anything."

"Thanks for the vote of confidence," I said.

"This from the guy who once forged his mom's signature on a failed test and spelled her name wrong."

"Shut up." I was in grade three when that happened. Would she never let me forget it? "I need to do this by myself," I said.

Shard stared at me for a moment and then shrugged. "No probs. I'll wait with Uncle Vinnie."

Dawson City was much smaller than I'd imagined. We drove past a gas station that had a small garage attached to it as we came into town on the Klondike Highway. Vinnie did a quick stop, and he and Fiona went in to see if Lefty could fix her Ducati.

We helped Fiona unload the bike and both Shard and I pretended not to see the little hug Vinnie gave her before he climbed back in the truck. We continued on into the town, looking for the Mining Recorder Office on Front Street.

It turned out to be a two-storey building with brown siding and big wooden double doors.

"The Bonanza Market is a few blocks over on 2nd Avenue, according to Fiona," Vinnie said. "We're gonna grab some lunch and load up on supplies."

"I'll meet you there when I'm done," I said, hopping out of the truck expecting Shard to beg to come along. She didn't.

I walked up to the building and froze. Now that I was here, I wasn't sure I could go through with it. I sat on the step outside the office and pulled my granddad's picture from the pack. His face in the picture looked solemn, like he was trying to tell me something. The Dearing sour luck.

Maybe it was time for it to end.

"Isn't dat Wally Dearing?" a voice asked.

I looked up in shock to see a man towering over me. His eyes were almost hidden by blondish-grey bangs that were so uneven they could have been cut with a chainsaw. His hair was long and straight and he had the same coloured beard. He looked like a Viking straight out of a book.

I put the picture back in my backpack. "No. It's just a souvenir," I lied. I didn't need any more people knowing what I was doing.

"So, are you coming or going?" He pointed at the door behind me.

That was the question, wasn't it? Was I coming or going? I took a deep breath. Chris Dearing might be too scared to turn things around, but Dirk Stark would be bold, wouldn't he?

"Coming."

He smiled and nodded. "Then you should be on your feet and pointed in the other direction, heh?"

I forced myself to my feet, walked to the door, pulled on the handle and went in. He followed me inside.

There were a couple of men at the tall wooden counter already, talking to the registrar. The Viking man went over to a table by the wall that had trays of forms on it. He sat down in the nearby chair and began filling one out.

I stood behind the two men. They were talking about the river — how high it was last week, how low it was last year, how many boats they saw on it yesterday, how fast it was running this spring and how small the fish were this year.

I tried hard not to fidget.

They moved on to talking about the town dump — how big it was getting, the bear that was spotted there last week, the treasure they found there by digging through the piles, and on and on.

The Viking finished filling in his form and stood up. "This young man has some business here, I think," he said.

The three men went silent and turned and stared at me. The two moved away from the counter.

"Sorry, Neils, we didn't see him there."

Whoever this Viking guy was, he seemed to be well known.

"Yes," the registrar said, glancing nervously at Neils. "What can I do for you?"

"I need some claim tags." My voice came out in a squeak.

"Claim tags, eh? You thinking of staking a claim?" The two guys who had been talking to him laughed out loud at that.

"Just helping out my dad," I said, worried that he wouldn't give them to me because I was so young.

"Two bucks." He handed me two small metal tags and a map of the area with the claims marked on it.

"Here's a pamphlet with instructions so your dad knows how to properly place the tags."

"Uh, thanks." I left the building and looked at the instructions outside. I had to fix the tags with nails, not wire, to a post or a tree with a flat side. I needed to make a trip to a hardware store.

"So, does your father know what to do?" It was Neils again. I don't know how a guy that big managed to keep sneaking up on me.

"I think so, but he'll need some tools. Do you know where there's a hardware store around here?"

"Sure, the Trading Post is just down the street."

"How far?" I asked.

"I'll show you. I need a new axe handle anyway."

I followed Neils. Or I should say, I tried to. He took such long strides I had to almost jog to keep up with him.

"So, what is your name?"

A simple question like that shouldn't catch you off guard. But it did.

"Dirk," I said. I already told him that the picture wasn't Wally Dearing — I couldn't very well now tell him I was Chris Dearing.

"Fine name!" Neils said. "Sounds like a strong Norse name. And your family name?"

"Stark."

"Stark? That doesn't sound Norse. Where is your father's family from?"

"Uh, Manitoba."

"Ah. But there must be some Norse in your background with a great name like Dirk, heh? I am Norse myself. Neils Amundson." He slowed long enough to hold out his hand. I shook it.

"Here we are, the Dawson Trading Post."

"Well, thanks for showing me, Mr. Amundson."

"Call me Neils."

We went in together. Neils was greeted by almost everyone in the shop. I guess that's what it was like when you lived in a small place.

I wanted to get in and out of there as fast as possible before Neils thought to ask me any more questions, like where my father was, where we live and what claim we wanted to register. I threw six nails in one of the little paper bags near the bin, and grabbed a cheap hammer and a hand saw. Luckily I had enough money to pay for it all, but just. I was down to under a dollar in change.

Outside, I hurried through a laneway back in the direction of the grocery store, to meet up with Vinnie and Shard so we could get going out to the claim.

As I rounded the corner onto 2nd Avenue by Nugget Nick's Café, I skidded to a stop. There was a police SUV parked next to Vinnie's truck and an officer was talking to him. I didn't see Shard anywhere.

I backed up slowly and crouched down behind the railing of the restaurant. What was I going to do now? I nearly jumped out of my skin when someone tapped me on the shoulder.

"Where were you?" Shard asked. "I've been waiting across the street from the Mining Recorder Office forever!"

"I had to get supplies at the hardware store. What happened with Vinnie?"

"He decided to sell a few leftover muffins from this morning and the cops came around asking about his licence. It went downhill from there."

"Oh, that's just great," I said. "How am I supposed to get out to the claim? I don't want to wait until tomorrow."

"I don't think you can."

"What do you mean?"

"I'm pretty sure I saw a familiar silver car parked in the Mining Recorder parking lot."

"Randy?"

Shard nodded. "I think so. You've got to get that claim staked pronto."

I pulled the claim map out of my pocket. "You know, it's not that far. I could probably walk it."

"Uh, what's the scale on this map?" she asked. "That might be farther than you think."

"I don't have much choice, do I?" I said. "Look, I'm going to start walking and when Vinnie has this all sorted out, you guys come to the claim and give me a ride back." I showed her the location of the claim on the map before folding it up and putting it back in my pocket.

"Aren't there dangerous wild animals out here?"

"More dangerous than Randy?" I asked. "Don't worry, I'll stick to the road."

Shard reached into the plastic bag she had slung over her arm. "Don't forget about the moose. They can trample you to death. Here, at least take these." She put two yellow balls in my hands.

"Onions?"

"Yes, onions. I heard they keep moose away. They hate the smell. Cut the onions open and stick them in your pockets."

"Where'd you hear that? And what about the bears?"

"They're busy picking berries in the woods. They don't want a stinky onion boy either."

I didn't have the energy to argue with her logic. I stuffed the onions in my jacket pockets, took one last look at Vinnie throwing his arms up in the air as he talked to the cops, and reminded Shard to come for me as soon as possible. She headed to the truck to see if she could help Vinnie. I needed to get going.

As I rounded a big bush on the corner of 2nd Avenue and King Street at a jog, I skidded to a stop. Again. Six more steps and I would have barrelled right into Enemy #1 — Randy. He was talking to a woman in a navy pantsuit carrying a briefcase.

"Yeah, I'm sure it's him," I heard Randy say to her. "I told Mrs. Ledbetter I'd notify the local child protective services if I saw him on my way up here. Here's her number."

"I'll give her a call, thanks," the woman said.

My heart thudded in my chest: he was talking to Enemy #2 — another caseworker. It was every nightmare I'd had in the past week come to life. Shard did say that she saw Randy talking to Mrs. Family Services in the apartment hallway before we left. A snake helping a piranha.

I crouched down behind the bush, trying to control my breathing so I wouldn't give myself away.

I didn't think things could possibly get worse.

I was wrong.

CHAPTER 22

TREED AND OUT OF ONIONS

I sneezed.

The bush in front of me was covered in little white flowers but as far as I knew, I didn't have allergies. But then I'd never been to the Yukon before. I peered through the branches, hoping a car or the wind or something, anything, had covered up the noise.

Nope.

Randy and Mrs. CPS were both staring in my direction. Then Randy started coming over to the bush.

I had no choice. I jumped up and ran.

With every ounce of energy I had left, I sprinted back toward Front Street — the opposite way from the claim. I could hear and feel Randy's heavy footsteps pounding on the dirt road behind me. I veered left on Front Street to where the Trading Post was because I knew the street was full of tourists. I was hoping I could shake him in the crowds. To the right of the Trading Post was a dirt alley. Ducking behind a group from a bus tour, I headed down the alley, back toward 2nd Avenue. I glanced over my shoulder and couldn't see Randy, which was a relief because I was spent. I came to a stop, gasping for breath.

Then I heard pounding again. I looked behind me and saw Randy coming down the alley. I took off up 2nd Avenue, past Vinnie's truck. Getting to King Street, I hung a right. Up the road there was a pub, Straggly Jack's, and behind it was a familiar sight — a Dumpster. I ducked behind it and waited. In a matter of seconds I heard footsteps go by, slow, and then stop. Then, every nerve in my body on alert, I heard the footsteps come closer, pause, and come closer still. I could feel a trickle of sweat roll down my back.

"What are you doing there, heh?"

It was Neils. I nearly fainted with relief. I barely had the strength to stand up.

"I thought you were someone else."

"Now who would you be hiding from? That's what you were doing, right? Hiding?"

"Uh, yeah. I thought someone was following me."

Neils put his hands in his jeans pockets and rocked back on his heels, staring at me. "You know, when I was a boy, I got into a lot of trouble. So, I have a good eye for it. I don't think that's the whole story."

He was right, but I wasn't about to tell him. I had to get out of there. I was running out of time, and the longer we stood there, the more chance that Randy or Mrs. CPS would find me.

"I really have to go, Mr. Amundson."

"Call me Neils, remember? And go where? Where is your father staying?"

You know how sometimes you get a light bulb moment and everything clicks into place? This was one of those times. "He's said he'd meet me at my granddad's cabin."

"What? Out on your claim?"

I nodded.

"And how were you planning on getting out there?"

"Walking."

Neils laughed a big, hearty laugh. "Walk? In bear country? You'd be lunch for some hungry mama bear within half an hour."

I shrugged like it didn't matter. But *of course* it mattered — it's just that I didn't have much choice. To go back to living in some seedy apartment in the city while my dad sank deeper and deeper into misery and drink was unthinkable.

"Where's your granddad's cabin?"

I gave him the directions I had memorized to get there.

"That's just one road east of my place and out where they say Wally Dearing found his gold. You might get lucky. Look, come with me, and I'll drop you off with your dad."

I couldn't turn that down. With both Randy and Mrs. CPS on the hunt for me, there was no way I would have been able to stay hidden while walking down some road in the wilderness.

I walked out from behind the Dumpster with Neils, looking nervously left and right. Neils watched me, but said nothing. As we walked down King Street to where Neils's truck was parked, a cop car came up beside us. My heart seized in my chest. Was I really going to come this far only to be nabbed now?

"Hey there, Neils," the officer called out the window.

"Hey, Carl. What's up?"

"Just wanted to let you know that we caught that nuisance bear that you saw near your place and relocated him."

"That's great news. Anna was pretty nervous going to the garden."

"Who's this?" the officer asked, giving a bit of a chin nod in my direction.

"Dirk here and his dad are going to be mining out Cottonwood Creek way."

The officer chuckled, "Maybe they'll find Wally Dearing's lost treasure." He and Neils laughed. I felt my stomach turn over. Obviously the Dearings were a joke here too.

The officer waved to Neils as he drove off.

"Are you cold?" Neils asked me.

"No. Why?"

"Because you're shaking."

He'd be shaking too, if he knew how close I'd come to being busted right then. If Child Protective Services had gotten to the police, I'd have been heading south already.

"Uh, yeah, maybe a little cold."

Neils looked at me, but said nothing. I climbed into his blue pickup and snapped the seat belt. As we drove out of town, I kept a sharp eye out for Randy or Mrs. CPS. All was quiet. Was I finally going to catch a break?

Within minutes, there was nothing but trees, trees and more trees. No houses, no farms, no power lines, nothing. It was a little eerie. Neils was telling me all about his wife, Anna, and how he had been gold mining all his life. He pointed out the gravel road that led to his property, and then the road went over a small bridge.

"That's Cottonwood Creek," he said, and turned right onto the next dirt road. I sat up a little and had my first look at the land. No surprise, it was mostly trees. There was a downed tree blocking the end of the lane, but you could still see a clearing with a small log cabin in the distance.

"You sure your dad's here?" Neils asked. "I don't see anyone around."

"Oh, he said if I got there first, I should just wait for him," I replied smoothly. "Thanks so much for the ride, Neils."

"If you need anything, we're just the next road over," he said, looking uneasy. I guess he didn't want to leave me there alone, but I smiled and waved and headed for the cabin. Eventually I heard his truck back down the lane.

The sun beat down on me, and here among the trees where there was no wind, it was actually warm. Worse than that, it was buggy. And I mean *buggy*. Mosquitoes were swarming and biting me all over. Their high-pitched whine was constantly in my ear, almost driving me crazy. When we were here to mine, we'd have to get some bug spray. Maybe barrels of it.

And there were these odd grunting and crashing sounds coming from the bush. It made me nervous. As dumb as it sounded when Shard gave them to me, I pulled the onions out and used my small saw to slice them in half. I put them back in my pockets and man, did they smell.

Now the trick was to find the posts that marked the claim and attach my new tags. I knew from reading the website before we left roughly where they should be, so I started working my way through the bush to find the "location line."

It took a while, but I finally found one post. The old tag was hanging by only one nail and it was hard to read the words etched on it. The date it was staked was illegible but I could make out the name of the staker: Jonah Stuckless. It felt awfully good to rip that tag off the post. I stomped it into the mud under my foot for good measure.

This is for you, you filthy rat, I thought. Then I used the saw to lop off the sapling beside it to create a new post with a flat face. I used two of my new nails and my mini hammer to attach the tag. With the marker in my backpack, I wrote Francis Dearing on the post. I felt better already.

The second post was supposed to be visible from the first, but a lot of the trees and shrubs had overgrown the area, making it hard to see. I used my hammer like a machete to bushwhack my way through. I kept a listen for Vinnie's truck. Where was he?

I'm sure I lost a pint of blood to the mosquitoes by the time I located the second post. I pried the old Stuckless tag off that one and threw it as far away as I could. I was rummaging around in my backpack looking for the second tag when I heard something. It sounded like huffing — really loud, low huffing. I froze.

There was a thumping and crashing coming closer and closer through the brush. What was it? And was it coming for me?

I cut another small post as quick as I could and banged the top nail to hold my second tag on it. The noise was getting closer. Whatever it was, it was heading in my direction. I was working on the bottom nail when I looked up and saw it. A big brown moose head. I didn't realize moose were so large. I always pictured them more like the size of deer, but this sucker was in the elephant-size zone. At least that's how it looked from where I was, crouched down, trying to nail a tag to a post. I took one last swing at the nail and then headed straight for the nearest spruce tree.

I didn't have much experience climbing trees. I could shimmy up a drainpipe like a rat, or use a skipping rope like a ninja, but there weren't a lot of trees that needed climbing in the city. Still, it's amazing what you can do with a thousand-pound lady moose coming at you. I knew it was a she because she didn't have any antlers.

I got off the ground, but was stuck on the second-lowest branch. Why weren't the onions working? Hanging on to the branch with one hand, I used the other to pull one of the onion halves out and wave it around.

I prayed it would get one whiff of the onion and take off, but the moose just kept coming closer. And even though I was up a tree, the moose was so tall she could still reach me with her big yellow teeth.

"Shoo. Shoo!" I said, waving one onion half at her.

She stepped closer to the tree. This was the end. I was about to be a moose meal. Her face reached up to me . . . she huffed . . . opened her mouth . . . and sneezed. Great gobs of moose snot hit my arms. It. Was. Disgusting.

How did I get in this mess — stranded up a tree, my pockets full of onions and moose snot running down my arm?

Then the moose's lips came up to my hand. She snatched the onion right out of it and started chewing. She loved it. So much for onions keeping moose away. When I saw Shard again, I vowed, I was going to strangle her.

The moose finished chewing and could no

doubt smell the other three pieces in my pockets. This was going to end badly if I didn't think of something fast.

I dug in my pocket for another onion and threw it a little bit away from the tree. The moose heard it hit the ground and lumbered over. I could hear the crunching as she devoured it. I grabbed another onion half. I threw it so it would land a little farther from my tree, but close enough so the moose could find it. It worked. She ambled over and hunted around in the grass for it. One more. I waited until she was almost done chewing so she would notice it fall. It landed with a thud, and like the onion-lover she was, she headed straight for it.

It was my best chance. I jumped down from the tree and took off for the road. I hoped the moose wouldn't chase me . . . I was out of onions.

CHAPTER 23
NOWHERE LEFT TO RUN

Have you ever tried to run in a straight line with nothing to steer by? Yeah, it's next to impossible. You always go in a big circle. Did you know that? I know that. That's because long after I should have hit the dirt road leading to the highway, I was hopelessly lost in brush and trees.

I tried using the sun to get my bearings like they do in adventure stories, but seeing as I have no idea how to do that, all squinting at the sun did was give me spots in front of my eyes. I thought it was getting lower in the sky. But does the sun ever set around here?

I had to make my best guess and keep moving so I headed in the direction I decided was west. Seeing as I knew Dawson was west of our property, all I had to do was head in that direction for, oh, you know, a week or two and I'd be there.

That is if I wasn't sucked dry by the mosquitoes or eaten by a moose or mangled by a grizzly.

I stopped thrashing through the forest and sat on a rock. I pulled out my granddad's picture.

Fine mess I'm in now, I told the photo. *I found your claim, but now I can't find my way out.* I don't know what I was hoping would happen. Maybe the ghost of my granddad would appear with an outstretched arm pointing the way.

No ghost, but while I sat there in silence, I could make out a low gurgling sound I hadn't heard while I was snapping twigs and crunching last year's leaves underfoot. Then it hit me. It was the creek! Cottonwood Creek! All I had to do was follow it and I would eventually come out by the bridge at the road.

I smiled at the picture before wrapping it in my sweater again and putting it away. Granddad had come through after all.

I headed in the direction of the gurgling and almost fell into the creek. Facing the sun, I went to the right, which should be north, and figured that would take me to the road.

It wasn't easy following the creek. There was no path and sometimes I veered away from the water to go around a thick stand of trees or boulders. I was afraid I would get lost again, but if I stopped and listened, I would hear the gurgling.

The sun was casting long shadows now so I quickened my pace. A wall of spruce trees blocked my way — I had to detour again. This time I could hear something else: heavy footfalls. Was it a moose or a bear?

Little did I know, it would have been better to be a moose or a bear — that's because it was something much, much worse. Out of the shadows of the trees stepped someone I had hoped never to see again.

Randy. I didn't wait around to ask him how he found me, or what he was doing here, or what he wanted, because at this point the reasons were unimportant. I just took off. Forget trying to follow the creek — that took too long. I just headed for whatever looked like a trail.

It was no use. Randy was bigger, faster and stronger than me. He caught up to me, put his big mangy paw on my arm and yanked me back.

"Not so fast, scrawny," he said, his bad breath making me gag.

"Let go of me!" I yelled, trying to twist out of his grip. He just gripped me tighter. We were told once, in a program at school called Street Smarts, that if a stranger grabbed you, you did whatever it took to get free — including fighting dirty. So I did. I spun around to face Randy and kneed him right *there*. Where it really hurts a guy.

Randy let go of me and fell to the ground, holding himself and moaning. And no, I didn't feel sorry for him at all.

I took off again, using his pain to get a head start.

I was looking over my shoulder nervously in the direction of the noise when I ran smack into a post. It hit my right temple and dazed me for a moment. I had run into my claim post. Literally.

At least I knew where I was again. The rest would be easy. I would follow my bushwhacked trail to the second post, and the laneway out of here was just beyond that. Finally something was going my way.

There was a thumping noise behind me. A shadow fell across the post as whatever made that noise moved into view. My heart stopped. I knew I spoke too soon about things going my way. I was a Dearing. Things *never* went my way.

Towering over me, with teeth bared and eyes glinting, was Randy. "Thanks for showing me where the posts for my new claim are, kid," he said. Man, I wanted to wipe that smirk off his face.

He jingled something in his pocket and then laughed as he pulled out some metal claim tags. He walked over to the post, set the tags on top and then used a fierce-looking hunting knife to pry my tag off and start banging one of his tags on with the handle of the knife.

He was stealing our claim! To have come this far only to have it ripped right out of my hands? I couldn't believe this was happening.

I tried to think of a plan — some way to stop him — but he was huge and had bulging muscles and I was a scrawny kid. I wondered if I could pick up a branch and hit him over the head or something, but he kept one eye on me the whole time.

It all looked hopeless. Until I smelled the onions. That could only mean one thing: mama moose was near.

Randy noticed the smell too. "Is someone having a barbeque?" he asked, sniffing the air. Then he saw something. "Don't look now, kid, but there's a ferocious wild animal coming to get you." He laughed and pointed. I looked to my right and saw a baby moose trying to navigate the bushes with his ridiculously gangly legs.

Randy was slapping his leg with laughter, but the hair on the back of my neck stood up. There is one universal truth about baby wild animals — admire them, take pictures of them, talk baby talk to them if you really have to, but never, NEVER come between a baby and its mama.

And that's exactly what Randy had done. The

baby was in front of Randy and the smell of onions was definitely coming from *behind* him. I took a sideways step away from the moose calf. I didn't want to be in the middle of that mess.

There was a snort and a stomp and suddenly Mama Onion-Breath came into view. She was not happy. In fact, her eyes were pinned on Randy with a look only a mother whose baby is in danger can have. I have to admit, I got a lump in my throat at the fierceness with which that mama was protecting her little one. Lucky baby moose.

I took another step out of the way. That moose looked even bigger now that I was on the ground and not in a tree. The calf bawled. Mama snorted. Randy started to sweat. He looked from the baby, to the mama, to the baby and back to the mama. She didn't even like him looking at her baby; she started charging. Randy took off toward the creek with mama hot on his heels. The baby staggered after them.

This was my chance to escape! I was about to sprint for the road when I saw them — Randy's tags. One was half on our post and the other was sitting on top. I could hear Randy yelling and the moose's footsteps pounding and the baby bawling, so they weren't that far away, but I had to fix this.

I ripped Randy's tag off. I found mine where it had landed on the ground and used my hammer to pound it back into its place on the post. Then I grabbed both of Randy's tags and took off toward the laneway.

I slowed down only once, when I was almost to the lane and there was wonderful black, swampy ground on my left. I tossed those tags as far into the murky water as I could and heard them splash. Then I sped up again, running as fast as my burning lungs would let me.

I was coming to the end of the lane; the main road was in sight. I prayed that Vinnie would be on his way with Shard. I heard an engine and crossed my fingers. But it wasn't Vinnie. It was the engine of Randy's car.

I got to the highway and took off down the road toward Dawson. It was no use. Randy caught up to me, slammed his car into park, hopped out and grabbed me. I was breathing so hard I couldn't even stand up straight.

"Not so fast, pipsqueak. Where are my tags?"

I forced myself up and looked him square in the eyes. "They're in the swamp."

Randy's face twisted in rage. "Then I guess you're going for a muddy swim, aren't you?"

Before I could answer, we heard another car coming.

"One word, just one word," Randy said in my ear, "and you'll regret it."

It was a cop. Can you believe that? Any other time I'd be thrilled to see a cop come and rescue me from a loony-tune like Randy, but this was jumping from one disaster to another. If I said nothing, I'd probably drown or die of hypothermia wading through the swamp, and then lose the claim. Or if I did say something, the police would haul me off to Child Protective Services.

"Remember what I said, kid," Randy said again, loosening his grip on my arm slightly and pasting his fake smile on his face.

The officer got out of his cruiser and came over to us. "Everything okay here?"

"Oh, sure, kid just needed to pee," Randy said.

"That right, son?" the officer asked me.

"No, it isn't. This guy is trying to kidnap me!"

That's right. I would rather go into foster care than lose the claim now. My dad still needed somewhere to go and something to do.

The officer looked to Randy, whose fake smile was replaced with a dark look. "Can I talk to you over here, sir?" he asked, pulling Randy away from me. "Do you have some ID on you?"

Randy was pulling his wallet out and shooting me looks of hatred.

I took a nonchalant step down the road.

"Stay right there, son," the officer said, noticing. "I need to speak to you next."

So much for making a run for it. My shoulders sagged. I was tired, cold and hungry. Where was Vinnie? Or Shard? Or even Fiona?

Randy's voice was getting louder and louder. The officer didn't seem to like that, so he opened the back door of his cruiser and made Randy get inside. Then he shut the door and spoke into the two-way radio on his shoulder. He nodded at whatever was said and walked over to me.

I heard the motor of another vehicle behind me, coming from the direction of Dawson. I couldn't see who it was because I was facing the cop, but it had to be Vinnie. All I had to do was stall for a few more minutes.

"So now I want you to tell me what happened," the officer said to me. "But first I need your name."

My name? Oh brother. What should I tell him? I almost didn't know anymore. Was I Chris, Dirk or Wally? I figured I had better stick with the same name I gave the other cop — Wally Marrien.

I opened my mouth to lie . . .

"His name is Christopher Dearing," a voice from behind me said.

I spun around. It wasn't Vinnie. It was Mrs. CPS holding up a file folder.

"And he's a runaway," she added.

The cop looked back at me. I shook my head, but tears were pricking at the corners of my eyes. I couldn't believe it was going to end like this. With Randy stuck in the cop car and my tags still on the claim posts, all I had to do was get to town and tell Vinnie it was time to register the claim, and it was ours.

"Is that true?" the officer asked me.

I had to swallow a few times, my throat was so tight. "No, I'm not running away. I'm running to," I said.

"Running 'to'?" the officer asked, looking confused.

Mrs. CPS came closer. "He is a minor with no guardian, and he is under my jurisdiction," she told the officer.

"And who are you?"

"Mrs. Olsen, Family and Children's Services, Whitehorse," she said, handing him a card.

While the officer read her card, there was the sound of yet another engine. This time it was a pickup coming out of the Amundsons' lane.

The pickup pulled over to where we were standing and Neils got out. It was ridiculous the number of vehicles stopped in the road in the middle of nowhere, and not one of them was Vinnie's.

"What's going on here, Mark?" Neils asked the officer.

"Hi, Neils," the officer said. "Just sorting it out."

"Is the boy in trouble?" Neils asked, looking over at me.

"He's a runaway."

"Dirk," Neils said, "is this true?"

"His name is Christopher," Mrs. Olsen repeated.

Neils looked at me, confused. "I thought you said your name was Dirk?"

I shook my head. Now the tears flowed and I could do nothing to stop them.

The officer looked at me sternly. "Was that man really trying to kidnap you?"

I guess now that I had been caught in one lie, everything I said was questionable. I nodded.

"He followed me up here. He's a pickpocket. He threatened me."

The officer made a note on his notepad. "Threatened you with what?"

"He's trying to steal our claim. He ripped my tag off the post and tried to put his own on. He told me he was going to put me in the swamp."

The officer looked back at the cruiser with Randy in the back, his face pressed against the window, black with anger.

"Well, he certainly is bad news," the officer said. "I've run his name. He has outstanding warrants and he's under arrest. He'll be kept overnight in Dawson and then flown back to Whitehorse to face charges."

Then the officer looked at me. "And what about you? What is your real name? No lying now."

"Chris Dearing," I said, hating every syllable.

"You're a Dearing?" Neils said, his mouth open in surprise. "So that's why you came to Cottonwood Creek? You're a relative of Wally's?"

"He was my grandfather," I said.

"Why didn't you say so?" Neils asked.

I didn't answer. I was done talking. I couldn't explain to him how it felt to be a Dearing, and how much I wanted to get away from that name, how embarrassed I was by it all.

"So, what do we do with you now?" the officer asked, folding his arms.

"He's coming back with me," Mrs. Olsen said.

"To go where?" the officer asked. "You certainly can't start driving back to Whitehorse tonight. You'll hit a moose or a caribou for sure, and that's if you don't end up driving off the road."

"Well," Mrs. Olsen stammered, "I, um, will have to get a room, I guess, and I'll have to sleep outside his door so I can make sure he doesn't take off overnight."

"A room? Tonight? Are you kidding?" Neils said. "It's the annual Top of the World Highland Games. There isn't a room available in the entire district."

"Well, could you hold him overnight?" she asked the cop.

"I'm not locking a kid up," he said quickly.

Really? I thought that was the first thing he'd want to do. Maybe they grew cops differently up here.

Mrs. Olsen stammered some more. The cop folded his arms. Randy was pounding on the window of the cruiser and yelling something no one could make out.

"I have the solution," Neils said. "You can both stay with Anna and me. We have plenty of room."

"Will it be secure?" Mrs. Olsen asked, suspicion in her voice.

"If you are asking if Dir . . . I mean, Chris, will run away, I think the answer is no, heh?" Neils said, looking at me with his eyebrows raised.

I looked at the ground. "I have nowhere left to run."

"So, it's settled," Neils said. "Let's get out of the cold night air. Anna has a fine stew ready."

"Thanks, Neils," the officer said. "I'll take care of this one." He gestured back at Randy.

I climbed in Neils's pickup truck. No way I

was getting in Mrs. Olsen's car. We didn't speak all the way down the laneway to his house.

There was nothing left to say.

CHAPTER 24

WITH A WAVE OF HIS HAND

I didn't want to open my eyes. Once I opened them, I'd have to face the day. If I kept them closed I could stay wrapped in this cocoon of mountain-fresh-smelling sheets and forget the mess I was in.

I heard the knob turning and a squeak as the door opened a bit. "So, Christopher, breakfast is ready," a soft voice said from outside my door. It sounded like Neils's wife, Anna, who I had met only briefly the night before as she kept refilling my bowl with stew. "Christopher?"

I sighed and opened my eyes. Anna had stuck her head in and was smiling at me. I smiled and gave a little wave of understanding. It wasn't her fault my life was a chaotic mess.

I dragged myself out of bed and put on some clothes from my backpack. No hope of avoiding the horrors of foster care and a lost claim,

I guess. This is where Shard would tell me to quit whining already. I wondered where she was and if she was worried about me because I never came back to town. Did she sleep in the truck on the flour sacks again last night? Was Fiona's bike fixed? Was Vinnie in trouble with the cops? It felt as if I had been away from them for days, not hours.

I made my way down the hallway to the kitchen, which smelled like pancakes. My mouth watered at the thought of them. Just beyond the kitchen was an eating area with a full wall of windows overlooking a neat yard with a little gazebo in the middle. It had a garden gnome pecking out of the flowers around it. I hate garden gnomes; they give me the creeps.

Around the table sat Neils, Anna and Mrs. Olsen. They seemed to be deep in conversation when I arrived but they all stopped talking and looked up when I came in. Anna pulled out a chair for me next to her and pointed to a stack of pancakes in the middle of the table.

"The ones on the top are chocolate chip," she said. "And there is real maple syrup here in this jug."

I know it was rude of me not to even say good morning to anyone, but I wasn't in a polite mood. My life was about to go down the toilet, so they would just have to forgive me for not being social.

I took one pancake and put it on my plate. I was planning on eating just the one, but I have to tell you, that thing was so soft and tasty and warm, and the syrup was so yummy, that I took one after another after another until there was only one pancake left on the plate.

"So you said your family has been mining here for a long time, Neils," Mrs. Olsen said.

"Yup, for the better part of a hundred years. Almost as long as his family," he said, nodding his head in my direction.

"It must be a hard life," she went on.

"Well, a little hard, but good honest work never did anyone any harm."

Then Mrs. Olsen turned to me. "And why is it our department had to chase you all the way up here, Christopher?"

I just shook my head. There was no use in trying to explain it all. She would never understand.

"I think he wants to be a miner like his grandfather," Neils said. "Get the old Dearing claim back."

"Is that right?" she asked me. "You think you can mine a gold claim at your age?"

"Not by myself," I said. "With my dad." I lifted

my head and stared at her, daring her to say something bad about him.

"And he knows about this plan? He wants to come up here and mine?"

I nodded.

She sighed. "So why isn't this in the file? Did you tell your caseworker about these plans? Maybe we could have helped."

"You didn't want to help," I said, really holding back the tears now. "You just wanted to put me in foster care."

"Christopher, we are not in the business of breaking up families; we try to keep them together. But whether you like it or not, your dad was going to jail and there was no one to look after you. At least temporarily. And you deserve to be looked after."

"I don't need any help."

She sighed again. "Everyone needs help at some time or another. The idea of foster care was to give you a place to stay until your dad got on his feet again. If we had known about this gold mining thing, maybe we could have worked something out. But now . . ."

"But now what?" Neils broke in. "The boy and his father are trying to make a go of it. Miners have been coming up here for hundreds of years with a lot less than they have."

"Yes, but he's underage. He can't just squat up here waiting for his father to get his act together."

"No, he can't," said Anna, pulling herself up straight. "But he can stay here with us."

Neils slapped his hand on the table so hard that the syrup jug jumped. "Yes, of course he can."

I looked up in surprise. Would they do that for me after I lied about my name and why I was up here? I could be right next door to our claim!

"No he can't," Mrs. Olsen said.

Leave it to her to suck the life out of everything.

"Why not?" Anna asked.

"Because you aren't certified foster parents."

Neils made a *pfft* noise. "So certify us. We raised five kids of our own and they're doing fine. Everyone in Dawson knows me if you need references."

"It takes more than that. You have to apply, then there are interviews and a mandatory course . . ."

Neils waved a hand. "You can fix all that. In the meantime, the boy can stay here."

Mrs. Olsen was getting red in the face. "You can't just wave your hand and become foster parents . . ."

Neils leaned across the table, putting his face

close to hers. "He's just going to run away from wherever you drag him and come back here again. If you are serious about helping him and his dad, this is where he needs to be." He slapped his hand on the table to reinforce his point. Then he got up and went out the back door into the yard, whistling. I guess the meeting was over.

Mrs. Olsen finished her coffee and looked at Anna. "I'll see what I can do." Anna just smiled and nodded. I got the feeling Neils got his way a lot.

Mrs. Olsen went into the room where she had slept and closed the door. Did anyone notice that I hadn't been asked what I wanted?

"You know, if you hurry and find Neils before he gets started on some project, I'm sure he'd run you into town to register that claim," Anna told me.

My head snapped up. The claim! I had forgotten it hadn't been registered. I had the tags on, but now I had to do the paperwork. I ran to the room where my backpack was and pulled out my granddad's picture. I undid the back . . . but there was no registration form. What happened to it?

Then I remembered. Back in the truck when we were practising forging my dad's name, Fiona had handed me back the receipt but not the form.

"I need to get to Lefty's garage," I said to Anna,

who was finishing her coffee. I hoped the Ducati was still there and that Fiona wasn't already on her way home, taking the precious signed document with her. Forging a new document was out of the question — I didn't want anything that would make the registration invalid.

"What do you want with that place?" Anna asked.

"Nothing. It's just the form I need is with a, um, friend of mine who was getting her motorbike fixed there."

Anna looked at me with a funny look on her face. "Who is this friend?"

"Her name's Fiona."

"Fiona who drives a motorbike? Is it some fancy schmancy thing?"

Now I was starting to worry. "Yeah," I said slowly.

"Well, well, well. I wondered when Fiona Stuckless would show up back here."

Honestly, every blood cell in my body came to a screeching halt. "Fiona who?"

"Stuckless. She's the only Fiona I know who races around on a motorbike." Anna got up from the table and began clearing it. I was rooted to my spot.

I was stupid, that's what. And gullible. But mostly stupid. Shard was right, as usual — no one takes a kid on a long trip like this just as some kind of favour to someone. Without the form my dad signed, I couldn't register the claim. All Fiona had to do was get her own tags, stake the claim and register it. And she would, because Fiona was a Stuckless — the daughter of one of the swindlers, Jonah Stuckless: a no-good, low-down, filthy rat. And now the very family that had robbed ours years ago had the power to do it again. Why, oh why, did I forget to get that form back?

I was a Dearing, all right.

CHAPTER 25
WHEN THE LUCK RUNS OUT

Neils didn't say much as we drove along. I figured it was because he was still pretty upset about my lying about my name. I didn't feel like talking anyway — my stomach was in knots.

We pulled up in front of Lefty's garage. The bay doors were open but I couldn't see anyone around. I also couldn't see the Ducati anywhere.

"You sure this is the right place?" Neils asked.

"Yeah, but maybe she's gone already."

"And you say she has the paper you need?"

I nodded and got out to speak to the guy I finally found out back.

This trip was a waste of time. The Ducati was fixed yesterday and Fiona was gone. I got back in the pickup and slumped in the front seat.

Neils got back on the road into town. Maybe Fiona had gone there looking for Vinnie. It was my only hope.

We turned onto 2nd Avenue and I held my breath. Then I let it out again — there was no Ducati in sight. I wish I could say I was surprised, but I wasn't. After all, she was a Stuckless. I had to find out where she was, and there was one person who could help me: Vinnie. As if on cue, I saw a guy coming toward the truck with a familiar muffin box in his hands.

I jumped out of the truck. "Excuse me," I said, and the man stopped. "Do you know the Muffin Man?"

"The Muffin Man?"

"The Muffin Man!" I said, pointing at his box.

"Oh, yes, I know the Muffin Man, he's parked on Deadman's Lane."

"Thanks!" I hopped back in. Neils had the truck started already.

"What's a muffin man?" Neils asked.

"Friend of mine."

It only took a few minutes to make our way over to Deadman's Lane. When I saw the food truck, I have to admit, I choked up a bit.

I ran to the back of the truck, where the doors were open and Vinnie was inside. I could tell, because he was singing Italian opera in a terribly off-key voice. No wonder he had been arrested for doing it in an intersection for money — he was a horrible singer.

"Well, there you are," Vinnie said, seeing me. "We were worried about you when we couldn't meet you at the claim. What happened to you?"

"My luck ran out," I said.

"Shoot. What a day. So did mine. Got sidelined for not having a business licence. They took away my keys an' everything."

So that's why Vinnie never came for me. I knew something had to have happened — Vinnie didn't seem the type to not keep his word.

"What will you do?" I asked.

"Well, I made enough money in Whitehorse to pay for a licence but not the fine, but the people around here are real accommodating. They are allowing me to work off what I owe by selling my muffins."

"So, you'll be around Dawson for a while?"

"Looks that way." He gave one of his famous smiles. "Well, back to work. I can barely keep these Nugget muffins in stock."

This was good news. Vinnie would still be around to pretend to be my dad.

"Uh, Vinnie, where's Shard?"

"Oh, she went to the store for more supplies. She'll be back soon."

"And Fiona?"

Vinnie bent down to take a new batch of muffins out of the oven. "Fi's gone to take her uncle to some river. I'm not sure why. Maybe they're fishing."

No, they weren't fishing. Uncle Joey was finally going to his resting place. This was good news. At least Fiona wasn't motoring down the highway already.

"Did she say if she was coming back here?"

Now I saw something I never expected to: Vinnie was blushing. "Um, yeah, she said she'd come back to say goodbye." He bent down quickly to put more trays in the oven.

I turned to ask Neils if he minded if I waited for her for a while but I was stopped by a familiar face right in front of me.

"Way to ditch us, loser."

You know, despite her sharp tongue, I was really happy to see Shard. "Ditch *you*?" I said "How about you abandoning me? First I was attacked by Randy, who was trying to steal my claim, then the cops started interrogating me, and then Child Protective Services caught up to me."

Shard was quiet for a moment. "Okay, you win. Your day was worse than mine."

You're darn right I won. Or lost. Depends how you look at it.

"So, how did you get away from Mrs. Child Snatcher?" Shard asked, looking around.

"Mrs. Olsen. I didn't."

"Then . . . ?"

"Neils and Anna said that I can stay with them."

"Who are they?"

"They have the claim next to my grandfather's."

"And this Mrs. Olsen went for it?" Shard asked, looking skeptical.

"Well, Neils didn't give her much choice. I'll still be in foster care, but at least I can stay and be close by when my dad gets here. What about you? With your uncle here for a while, will you stay too?" I tried really hard not to sound too eager, but I was. It's hard starting over in a new place with no friends.

"Can't. My folks are bugging me to get back, so Fiona's going to give me a lift home."

Fiona! I had to find her and see if she still had my form or if she had conveniently "lost it."

"Did Fiona say where she was going to meet you?"

"Right here, in about . . ." She looked into the truck at Vinnie's clock on the wall. ". . . fifteen minutes. Said she had to dispose of her uncle Joey. I guess he's floating down the river by now."

I went over to the pickup truck to let Neils know I was waiting a few minutes, and he told me he was going to nip over to the gas station to fill up. It felt good to be trusted again, even if only for a few minutes.

"So, when are you leaving?" I asked Shard while we waited, sitting on the edge of the wooden sidewalk near Vinnie's truck.

"As soon as Fiona gets here."

We sat in silence. I wondered what it was going to be like without her being just down the hallway. Maybe Neils had a computer and we could email or something. Still, it wouldn't be the same.

"Oh, here. I meant to give you this." She handed me a piece of paper.

A receipt . . . for onions? "So was that some sort of a joke?" My voice rose to almost a yell.

"What are you talking about?"

"Those onions!" I waved the receipt in front of her face. "They nearly got me killed! Onions don't repel moose; moose LOVE them! I had one slobbering all over me trying to get them out of my pockets."

"Settle down. If the moose was eating the onions, then it wasn't eating you, right? So they worked. Get over it already."

How do you argue with that?

"Turn it over, doofus," she said, pointing at the paper. On the back was her phone number.

"Just in case you lost the other paper I gave you with my number and thought you had an excuse not to call me."

I tried not to grin, but I couldn't help it. I slipped the onion receipt into my pocket. "Thanks," I mumbled.

Over the sound of a man ordering half a dozen Breakfast Bonanza muffins, we heard it: the purr of the Ducati.

Fiona stopped and took off her helmet. She went straight into the back of Vinnie's truck, and I could see that the lineup of people waiting for their orders wasn't moving. Seems business had come to a halt. I didn't want to know what they were doing in there.

After a few minutes, Fiona came out, a little bit flushed. I pulled myself off the sidewalk and walked over to her. Maybe I was wrong about her. Maybe she didn't have an ulterior motive for bringing me up here. Maybe she was from a different Stuckless family.

"Hi, Fiona. Say, have you still got that paper with my dad's signature on it? I need it."

"No, I don't."

Okay, so I wasn't wrong about her. "Are you sure? I really need it." I was giving her one more chance.

She snapped on her helmet. "What do you

need it for? It's no good to you; you can't pretend to be old enough to register a claim. They would have laughed you out of the office," she said. "Come on, Shard. We're going to lose daylight."

Shard looked at Fiona in astonishment. "That's it? You're just going to leave him with this mess?"

Fiona climbed on the Ducati. "I don't have time to argue this. If you want a ride back, Shard, get on."

Shard's hand balled into a fist. I shook my head. It was over and if Shard started anything with Fiona, she'd be walking back. Reluctantly, Shard grabbed the other helmet strapped to the back and put it on.

"See ya, Chris," Shard said, climbing on. "Remember to call." She gave a wave as Fiona started up the Ducati and then hung on for dear life as they took off down the street.

I was stunned. In only a matter of seconds, it seemed, everything I had worked for was gone. Fiona had no intention of giving me back the registration form. I hung my head. The Dearing luck was as black as ever — we had been thwarted again.

CHAPTER 26

ONCE A DEARING ...

I sat back down on the sidewalk to wait for Neils, although I don't know why I bothered. I didn't have the claim anymore and it would be absolute torture to be living beside it, seeing someone else living in my granddad's cabin and mining our claim. Maybe I should just head south again. Then at least in the fall I could go back to my old school, and Shard would be just down the hall again if I could talk Critch into getting our old place back.

Neils's pickup pulled up beside me and stopped. I hopped in.

"Said your goodbyes?" he asked. I nodded. "Where to next?"

"Nowhere," I said, dejected.

"Don't you want to check out some equipment while we're here? If I'm going to teach you mining, you'll need the basic tools."

"Don't bother. I won't be mining. I'll probably be heading back south as soon as possible."

Neils pulled the truck over to the side of the road. "What are you talking about?"

"Fiona Stuckless and the swindled claim."

"Sounds like a novel."

"Worse. It's real life."

"Tell me what happened."

So I told him — the truth this time. I told him about my granddad and how he was swindled by Jonah Stuckless and Ben Odle. About how my dad had kept a signed registration form behind the photo. And about how I was so stupid that I forgot to ask for it back from Fiona.

"Are you sure she destroyed the form?"

"Of course she did. She's a *Stuckless*."

"True, but just in case, I want to stop in at the Mining Recorder Office."

"Waste of time," I said, looking out the window.

Neils drove to Front Street and parked in front of the now-familiar brown building.

"Come on," he said.

All I could hope was that Fiona threw the form away and not that she registered it for herself. Then maybe I could somehow get a new form for my dad to sign.

"Hiya, Dave," Neils said to the guy behind the

counter. "I need you to do me a favour. Can you check the status of the old Dearing claim? I'm not sure what the number is . . ."

"Everyone knows the Dearing claim," Dave said with a chuckle. "But I just came on duty, so give me a minute to do a search. Pete worked this morning and he's new in town, so heaven only knows what kind of mess everything is in."

It felt like forever waiting for Dave to search for information on our claim.

"Well, looks like it's active."

"Active?" I asked.

"Yup, was just registered today."

I was speechless. Fiona sure worked fast. And now my dad and I were homeless and jobless.

I turned to leave. I wanted to go somewhere and cry. Or throw up. Or both.

"Who registered it?" I heard Neils ask Dave as I reached the door.

"Francis Dearing."

I froze.

"Who?" I asked, turning back around.

"It says Francis Dearing."

"Thanks, Dave," Neils said and pushed me out the door.

Outside I wiggled out of his grasp. "Wait," I said. "I don't understand. Is my dad here?"

"No, Mrs. Olsen said the earliest he can get out is three weeks from now."

"So, how did this happen?"

"Fiona must have put your form in."

"How could she . . . she's a girl. She couldn't pretend to be my dad."

"True. But you're forgetting that Francis is also a woman's name. My best guess is that she registered it for you."

My head started to pound as I tried to process everything. "Are you telling me that the claim is ours? That Fiona didn't swindle us?"

"Sure looks like it."

"But she's a *Stuckless*!"

"Yes, but she's not her dad," Neils said, putting a hand on my shoulder. "And neither are you."

We drove back out to Neils's house, where Anna was waiting with sandwiches. The bread was homemade and cut into thick slices. In between was a slab of ham.

Mrs. Olsen was out but drove back in the afternoon. Then she and Neils and Anna all sat together in the sunroom doing interviews and intake applications. I stayed outside, far away from them, and explored the area around the house. Don't get me wrong, I was grateful that Neils and Anna were taking me in, but the thought of being a foster child still made me queasy.

I wandered out behind the shed and followed a path a short way through the trees to a clearing, then stopped. A miniature village of tiny houses dotted the field. My first thought was, someone tell me this isn't for garden gnomes. Then a nose appeared at the open door of one of the houses. It was followed by a white snout, two dark-brown eyes, a black forehead and two pointed ears.

They weren't gnome homes; they were dog-houses and this was a sled dog!

He was beautiful. Soon other noses poked out of the other houses. I went from doghouse to doghouse petting them all and laughing as they jumped up and yipped at me. I wondered if Neils would let me learn how to run a sled this winter.

I waited around with the dogs until I heard Mrs. Olsen drive away and Anna called me for supper. We were having chicken fajitas. I had forgotten what it was like to eat three meals a day. At this rate, I'd need all new clothes by the time my dad made his way north.

As I got ready for bed, I went to the window of my new room and looked out. I can't tell you how it felt to watch the golden rays of the sun light up the tops of the spruce trees on the Dearing claim.

It seemed strange to think that it was back in our hands after all this time, but I had a feeling that the "loser Dearing" label was gone for good. My dad would come soon and get to work finding that pay streak and making our fortune. No one would snicker at the name Dearing again.

Maybe I'd hang on to the name after all.

ACKNOWLEDGEMENTS

Inspiration for this story came from watching too much TV — namely, shows about gold mining in the Yukon. Writing a book is a lot like gold mining. You don't know what you're going to come up with until you start digging, and in the end, you try to make something beautiful with what you find. I am very lucky to have supportive, talented people helping me dig and polish. Thank you to beta readers Christie Harkin, Hélène Boudreau and Lisa Dalrymple for their insightful comments and feedback. Thanks to Aldo Fierro for the awesome cover design, Erin Haggett's eagle eye and the whole team at Scholastic for their care and attention to every aspect of this book. Thanks to my wonderful editor, Anne Shone, for her talent, wit and charm, which went a long way in making this an enjoyable experience. Thanks always to my first reader, Chelsey, for her encouragement and unwavering belief in me and also for giving me the opportunity to try my hand at gold panning. To Alex, Nathan and Haley for cheering me on and helping me celebrate every small step along the way. And to Craig, for his photographic skill in capturing me at my best and his willingness to pick up the slack at home while I am talking to imaginary people.

ABOUT THE AUTHOR

Natalie Hyde is the acclaimed author of more than seventy fiction and non-fiction books for children, including *Saving Armpit*, *I Owe You One* and *Cryptic Canada: Unsolved Mysteries from Coast to Coast*.

She lives in southern Ontario with her family, a little leopard gecko, and a cat that desperately wants to eat him.